LONG-DISTANCE LOVE IN NEW YORK

Long-Distance Love in New York

Love Stories Around the World, Volume 4

Mikey Katodiya

Published by Mikey, 2024.

LONG-DISTANCE LOVE IN NEW YORK

First edition. April 30, 2024.

ISBN: 979-8224958030

Written by Mikey Katodiya.

This book is dedicated to those who dare to chase their dreams, embrace love's challenges, and find joy in life's little moments. May Alex and Sophia's story remind you that no distance is too great, no dream is too ambitious, and no love is beyond reach.

MIKEY KATODIYA

Foreword

In the intricate dance of life, love weaves a tapestry of emotions, experiences, and connections that shape our journey in profound ways. "Long-Distance Love in New York: Alex and Sophia's relationship is tested by distance as they pursue their dreams in the Big Apple" is not just a love story; it's a symphony of moments, a journey of growth, and a testament to the enduring power of love.

Within these pages, you will embark on a heartfelt journey with Alex and Sophia, two souls intertwined in the vibrant tapestry of New York City. Their love story is not without challenges, as distance tests the strength of their bond and life's twists and turns add layers of complexity to their path.

From the bustling streets of the Big Apple to the quiet moments of introspection, each chapter unfolds like a brushstroke on a canvas, painting a picture of love's resilience, resilience, and unwavering commitment. You will laugh with them in moments of joy, cry with them in moments of sorrow, and root for them as they navigate the complexities of life and love.

As you turn the pages, you will witness the evolution of their relationship, the growth of their characters, and the deepening of their connection. Themes of trust, communication, resilience, and the beauty of shared experiences resonate throughout, reminding us of the timeless truths that define meaningful relationships.

This book is not just a story; it's an invitation to explore the depths of human emotions, to celebrate the highs and lows of love's journey, and to find inspiration in the resilience of the human spirit. It's a reminder that love knows no bounds, transcending distance, challenges, and time itself.

So, dear reader, I invite you to immerse yourself in the pages that follow, to walk alongside Alex and Sophia as they navigate the twists and turns of their love story, and to discover the beauty of a love that endures, no matter the distance or obstacles faced.

May this journey resonate with your heart, ignite your imagination, and remind you of the timeless magic of love's embrace.

With love and anticipation,

Mikey Katodiya

Preface

In the realm of storytelling, every tale is a journey—a journey of discovery, of emotion, and of connection. "Long-Distance Love in New York: Alex and Sophia's relationship is tested by distance as they pursue their dreams in the Big Apple" is a narrative woven from the threads of real-life experiences, emotions, and the complexities of love.

This preface is not just an introduction; it's a glimpse into the heart of the story, a reflection of the journey that awaits within these pages. As the author, I have embarked on a creative voyage, exploring the depths of human relationships, the challenges of distance, and the resilience of the human spirit.

The characters, Alex and Sophia, are not merely figments of imagination; they are reflections of the people we encounter in our lives, the struggles we face, and the triumphs we celebrate. Their love story is a tapestry of moments—moments of laughter, tears, joy, and heartache—that resonate with the universal themes of love, loss, and longing.

Through their journey, you will witness the intricacies of long-distance relationships, the power of communication and trust, and the transformative nature of love in all its forms. Each chapter is a chapter of growth, a chapter of revelation, and a chapter of connection, as Alex and Sophia navigate the challenges of pursuing their dreams while staying true to their hearts.

As you delve into these pages, I invite you to not just read but to experience—to feel the emotions that stir within, to empathize with the characters' joys and sorrows, and to reflect on your own journey of love and resilience. This story is a mirror that reflects the complexities of human relationships, reminding us that love is a journey worth taking, even when the road ahead seems uncertain.

So, dear reader, I extend my hand and invite you to join Alex and Sophia on their journey—a journey of love, growth, and the enduring power of connection. May their story touch your heart, inspire your soul, and remind you that love knows no bounds, transcending time and distance to find its way back home.

With anticipation and warmth,
Mikey Katodiya

Acknowledgements

Writing a story is not a solitary endeavor; it's a collaborative effort fueled by the support, inspiration, and encouragement of many individuals. As I reflect on the journey of creating "Long-Distance Love in New York: Alex and Sophia's relationship is tested by distance as they pursue their dreams in the Big Apple," I am filled with gratitude for those who have played a part in bringing this tale to life.

First and foremost, I extend my heartfelt thanks to the characters of this story, Alex and Sophia, for allowing me to delve into their lives, dreams, and emotions. Their resilience, love, and unwavering spirit have been the guiding lights that shaped every word on these pages.

To my readers, thank you for embarking on this journey with me. Your support, feedback, and enthusiasm fuel my passion for storytelling, and I am honored to share this story with you.

A special mention goes to the vibrant city of New York, whose streets, sights, and sounds provided the backdrop for Alex and Sophia's love story. The city's energy, diversity, and spirit infused every scene with a sense of life and authenticity.

I am grateful to my family and friends for their unwavering support and belief in my creative endeavors. Your encouragement, love, and understanding have been invaluable throughout this writing process.

To my editor and publishing team, thank you for your dedication, guidance, and expertise in bringing this book to fruition. Your insights and attention to detail have truly enhanced the storytelling experience.

Last but not least, I express my deepest gratitude to the readers who have embraced Alex and Sophia's journey. Your connection with the story, your emotions, and your feedback inspire me to continue weaving tales that resonate with the human experience.

As I conclude this acknowledgements section, I am filled with gratitude for the privilege of storytelling and the opportunity to touch hearts, spark imagination, and celebrate the beauty of love and resilience. Thank you, from the bottom of my heart.

With love and appreciation,
Mikey Katodiya

Prologue

In the heart of New York City, where dreams are born and passions ignite, the story of Alex and Sophia begins—a tale of love tested by distance, of dreams pursued amidst challenges, and of the enduring power of connection.

Picture a city alive with energy, where skyscrapers touch the sky and streets buzz with the rhythm of life. It's in this vibrant backdrop that Alex and Sophia's paths first cross, two souls drawn together by fate and a shared ambition to chase their dreams in the Big Apple.

But like all great stories, theirs is not without its trials. As Alex dives into the world of finance, Sophia embraces the realm of art, each carving their path in a city that demands everything and gives nothing in return. The bustling streets become a metaphor for their relationship—filled with excitement, yet fraught with challenges.

As their careers flourish, so does their love. Late-night conversations, stolen moments in crowded cafes, and shared dreams under starlit skies weave the fabric of their bond. But as the city's pace quickens, so does the distance between them, testing the strength of their commitment and the depth of their love.

Through the highs of success and the lows of separation, Alex and Sophia navigate the complexities of a long-distance relationship. They learn the art of communication, the value of trust, and the importance of staying true to oneself while being there for the other.

Their love story is not just about romance—it's a reflection of the human experience, of resilience in the face of adversity, and of the unwavering belief that love can conquer all. It's a testament to the power of dreams, the beauty of connection, and the magic of finding your soulmate in the most unexpected of places.

As you embark on this journey with Alex and Sophia, I invite you to immerse yourself in the sights, sounds, and emotions of New York City. Feel the heartbeat of the city as it mirrors the heartbeat of their love, and discover that sometimes, the greatest love stories are born in the most challenging of circumstances.

So, dear reader, prepare to be captivated, inspired, and moved as you witness the love story of Alex and Sophia unfold against the backdrop of the city that never sleeps—a story that will touch your heart and remind you that true love knows no boundaries.

CHAPTER ONE

First Glance in the City That Never Sleeps

In the heart of New York City, where dreams danced along the skyscrapers and ambitions thrived in every corner, Alex and Sophia's story began. It was a typical morning in the Big Apple, with the sun casting golden hues over the bustling streets. Alex, a driven young artist, found himself lost in the maze of his latest masterpiece, capturing the city's energy on canvas. Meanwhile, Sophia, an aspiring writer, navigated through the crowded subway, her mind buzzing with ideas for her next novel.

Their paths intertwined at a quaint coffee shop tucked away from the chaos of Times Square. Alex, lost in his thoughts, bumped into Sophia as she entered, spilling her coffee and causing a momentary commotion. Apologies were exchanged, and as their eyes met for the first time, a spark ignited—an unspoken connection that hinted at a deeper bond yet to unfold.

Despite the rush of the city around them, Alex and Sophia found solace in each other's company. They shared stories of their dreams, fears, and aspirations, discovering unexpected similarities that drew them closer. As the day turned into night, they strolled through Central Park, the city's heartbeat echoing in their steps, and watched the skyline come alive with a mesmerizing display of lights.

Their first encounter was more than chance; it was a glimpse into a love story waiting to be written—a tale of two souls finding refuge in the chaos of New York, each bringing a piece of their dreams to the canvas of life.

As the chapter ends, a sense of anticipation lingers—a question of what destiny has in store for Alex and Sophia as they navigate their budding romance amidst the vibrant yet unpredictable cityscape of New York.

CHAPTER TWO
Whispers of Tomorrow's Promise

As days turned into weeks, Alex and Sophia's bond deepened amidst the vibrant chaos of New York City. Their love story unfolded like a delicate melody, each note resonating with hope, longing, and the promise of tomorrow.

On a crisp autumn evening, Alex surprised Sophia with tickets to a Broadway show—a whimsical escape from their hectic lives. The theater buzzed with excitement, and as the curtains drew open, they were transported into a world of romance and fantasy. The magic of the performance mirrored their own budding romance, weaving a tale of love, resilience, and the power of dreams.

After the show, they wandered through the city streets adorned with colorful autumn leaves. Sophia's laughter danced in the cool breeze, and Alex couldn't help but smile at the joy she brought into his life. They shared intimate conversations under the starlit sky, their hearts opening up like pages of an unwritten love story.

Amidst the enchanting backdrop of Central Park, Alex confessed his deepest feelings for Sophia, his words a melody of love and vulnerability. Sophia's eyes shimmered with tears of happiness as she reciprocated his affection, sealing their bond with a promise of forever.

As they embraced under the moonlit sky, a sense of serenity enveloped them—a fleeting moment frozen in time, capturing the essence of their blossoming love amidst the enchanting allure of New York City.

CHAPTER THREE
Echoes of Doubt in the Cityscape

As Alex and Sophia's love story continued to unfold against the backdrop of New York City's vibrant streets, whispers of doubt began to weave their way into their once-perfect world. The bustling energy of the city seemed to echo their inner turmoil as they navigated the challenges that tested the strength of their bond.

One rainy evening, as they walked hand in hand through Times Square, a sudden downpour caught them off guard. Seeking shelter in a nearby café, their conversation took a serious turn as doubts crept into their minds. Alex, consumed by the pressures of his artistic pursuits, expressed concerns about balancing his passion with their relationship. Sophia, equally driven in her writing endeavors, grappled with fears of losing herself in the whirlwind of New York's competitive landscape.

Their vulnerability laid bare, they confronted their insecurities with honesty and love. Through tears and whispered assurances, they reaffirmed their commitment to each other, promising to weather the storms together.

In the days that followed, they found solace in quiet moments amidst the chaos—a shared glance across a crowded room, a touch that spoke volumes of unspoken reassurance. Their love, though tested, grew stronger as they learned to navigate the ebb and flow of life in the city that never sleeps.

As the chapter drew to a close, a sense of resilience emerged—a testament to their unwavering determination to fight for their love amidst the challenges that threatened to pull them apart.

CHAPTER FOUR
Whispers of Change in the City's Rhythm

As the seasons shifted in the city that never sleeps, so did the rhythm of Alex and Sophia's love story. Change whispered through the streets, promising new beginnings and unexpected challenges that would test their resilience once more.

Amidst the bustling energy of a New York spring, Alex received an opportunity of a lifetime—a chance to showcase his artwork in a prestigious gallery. Excitement mingled with apprehension as he grappled with the prospect of success and the fear of losing himself in the spotlight.

Sophia, equally immersed in her writing journey, faced her own set of challenges. A deadline loomed for her latest novel, demanding every ounce of her creativity and dedication. The pressure to excel in a city where dreams were both nurtured and crushed weighed heavily on her shoulders.

As their individual pursuits took center stage, cracks began to form in their once-unbreakable bond. Late nights turned into early mornings spent apart, their conversations overshadowed by the weight of their ambitions. Misunderstandings brewed like storm clouds on the horizon, threatening to engulf the love they had fought so hard to preserve.

Yet, amidst the chaos of their changing lives, moments of clarity emerged. A stolen glance across a crowded gallery, a supportive gesture during a midnight writing session—small acts of love that spoke volumes of their enduring connection.

In a poignant moment beneath the cherry blossom trees of Central Park, Alex and Sophia confronted their fears and insecurities. They laid bare their hearts, acknowledging the challenges they faced while reaffirming their love for each other—a love strong enough to weather any storm, even in the ever-changing landscape of New York City.

As the chapter drew to a close, a sense of transformation lingered—a recognition that growth often comes hand in hand with adversity, and that true love endures, no matter the challenges it faces.

CHAPTER FIVE
Shadows of Doubt in the City's Glow

As the city's lights danced in the night sky, casting a mesmerizing glow over the streets of New York, Alex and Sophia found themselves grappling with shadows of doubt that threatened to dim their once-bright love.

The echoes of their individual pursuits reverberated through their shared moments, leaving behind a trail of unspoken worries and unmet expectations. Alex, basking in the acclaim of his art exhibition, felt the weight of external pressures seeping into his creative sanctuary. Sophia, amidst the final edits of her novel, struggled to find her voice amidst the cacophony of critical voices and self-doubt.

Their once effortless conversations now carried a tinge of hesitation, as they tiptoed around the unspoken fears that lurked beneath the surface. Late nights turned into silent dinners, punctuated by fleeting smiles that masked deeper concerns. The city's relentless pace mirrored their internal turmoil, pushing them further apart even as they yearned to hold onto each other.

A chance encounter at a rooftop bar offered a fleeting reprieve from their doubts. Beneath the starlit sky, amidst the city's skyline illuminated in a tapestry of colors, Alex and Sophia opened up about their struggles and fears. Their vulnerabilities laid bare, they found solace in shared understanding, their love a beacon of hope amidst the shadows that threatened to engulf them.

In a moment of clarity, they made a pact to confront their insecurities together—to embrace the highs and lows of their individual journeys while nurturing the love that bound them. As they watched the city shimmer in the night, a renewed sense of determination ignited within them, a promise to navigate the challenges ahead hand in hand.

As the chapter drew to a close, a glimmer of optimism pierced through the shadows—a reminder that even in the darkest moments, love has the power to illuminate the path forward.

CHAPTER SIX

Fragments of Hope Amidst the City's Chaos

In the midst of New York City's relentless chaos, Alex and Sophia sought fragments of hope to mend the cracks in their once-unbreakable bond. Their journey through the city's ups and downs had tested their love, but amidst the turmoil, glimmers of resilience and determination emerged.

As spring blossomed in the city, Alex found himself drawn to the tranquility of Central Park—a sanctuary amidst the urban jungle. Amidst the blooming flowers and serene landscapes, he sought clarity and solace, hoping to find answers to the questions that lingered in his heart.

Meanwhile, Sophia immersed herself in her writing, channeling her emotions into the pages of her novel. Each word became a cathartic release, a testament to her strength and resilience in the face of adversity. Yet, amidst the creative fervor, a sense of longing for connection tugged at her heartstrings.

Their paths converged once again in a chance encounter at a neighborhood bookstore. As they perused the shelves, lost in the world of literature, their eyes met—a silent acknowledgment of the unspoken emotions that bound them together. In that fleeting moment, amidst the aroma of old books and whispered conversations, they found a renewed sense of hope.

Over cups of steaming coffee at a nearby café, Alex and Sophia laid bare their hearts, sharing their dreams, fears, and aspirations. Their conversation flowed effortlessly, each word a bridge that bridged the gaps between them. They spoke of their struggles and triumphs, of the moments that tested their love and the ones that reaffirmed it.

As the evening sun painted the city in hues of gold, Alex and Sophia made a promise to each other—a promise to cherish the present, embrace the challenges, and build a future filled with love, laughter, and shared dreams. In that moment, amidst the city's bustling rhythm, they found fragments of hope that illuminated their path forward.

As the chapter drew to a close, a sense of optimism bloomed—a recognition that even amidst chaos, love has the power to heal, to mend, and to strengthen the bonds that hold us together.

CHAPTER SEVEN

Embracing Vulnerability in the City's Embrace

As the city's embrace grew warmer with the onset of summer, Alex and Sophia found themselves embracing vulnerability in their journey of love. Their experiences in New York had taught them that strength lay not only in resilience but also in the courage to be vulnerable with each other.

Amidst a sea of bustling tourists in Times Square, Alex and Sophia stole a quiet moment on a bench tucked away from the chaos. With the city's neon lights casting a surreal glow, they opened up about their deepest fears and insecurities. Alex spoke of his fear of failure, of not living up to the expectations placed upon him as an artist. Sophia, in turn, shared her anxieties about finding her place in the fiercely competitive world of literature.

Their shared vulnerability became a bridge that connected them on a deeper level. They found solace in each other's arms, embracing the imperfections and uncertainties that came with pursuing their dreams in the city they loved. In those moments of raw honesty, their love grew stronger, fortified by the understanding that they were not alone in their struggles.

As summer bloomed, they explored the city's hidden gems—quiet parks, rooftop gardens, and quaint cafés that offered refuge from the bustling streets. Each place became a canvas for their love story, a reminder that amidst the chaos, there were moments of tranquility and connection waiting to be discovered.

A spontaneous weekend getaway to the Hamptons provided a much-needed escape from the city's frenetic pace. Under the starlit sky, with the sound of waves crashing against the shore, Alex and Sophia danced to the rhythm of their hearts. In that intimate moment, surrounded by nature's beauty, they found solace in the simplicity of being together.

As the chapter drew to a close, a sense of acceptance permeated their relationship—a deep-rooted understanding that vulnerability was not a weakness but a strength that bound them together. In the city's embrace, amidst the hustle and bustle, Alex and Sophia found peace in being truly, authentically themselves with each other.

CHAPTER EIGHT

Navigating Crossroads in the City's Labyrinth

As the summer breeze swept through the streets of New York, Alex and Sophia found themselves at a crossroads in their journey of love. The city's labyrinthine paths mirrored the complexities of their emotions, as they navigated through uncertainties and pivotal moments that would shape their future together.

Amidst the vibrant energy of a street festival in Brooklyn, Alex and Sophia discovered a shared passion for music. They danced to the rhythm of live bands, their laughter mingling with the melodies that filled the air. In those carefree moments, they forgot the pressures and doubts that had weighed on their hearts, finding joy in the simple act of being together.

Yet, beneath the surface, questions lingered. Alex faced a critical decision regarding his art—a lucrative opportunity that could catapult him into the spotlight but came with sacrifices and compromises. Sophia, on the other hand, grappled with the realization that her dreams were evolving, leading her down unexpected paths she had never imagined.

Their conversations turned introspective as they explored their hopes and fears for the future. They spoke of their dreams as individuals and as partners, grappling with the delicate balance between ambition and love. In moments of vulnerability, they shared their doubts and insecurities, finding solace in each other's understanding and support.

A pivotal evening at a rooftop bar overlooking the city skyline brought their emotions to the forefront. Under the canopy of stars, Alex and Sophia bared their hearts, confronting the challenges that lay ahead. They acknowledged the fear of change, the uncertainty of what the future held, but amidst it all, they found courage in their love—a love that had weathered storms and emerged stronger.

As the night faded into dawn, a sense of clarity emerged—a recognition that life's crossroads were opportunities for growth and transformation. In the city's labyrinth, amidst the cacophony of voices and choices, Alex and Sophia found strength in their unity, ready to navigate the unknown together.

As the chapter drew to a close, a sense of anticipation lingered—a question of what paths they would choose and how their love would evolve as they stood at the threshold of new beginnings in the city they called home.

CHAPTER NINE
Harmony Amidst City's Symphony

As the city's symphony of life played on, Alex and Sophia discovered a newfound harmony in their relationship, weaving together the melodies of their dreams and aspirations. Their journey through New York had been a whirlwind of emotions, but amidst the chaos, they found moments of serenity and connection that strengthened their bond.

One summer evening, they stumbled upon a hidden jazz club in Greenwich Village—a dimly lit haven filled with soulful melodies and intimate vibes. The music spoke to their souls, resonating with the emotions they had kept tucked away. As they swayed to the rhythm of the jazz band, their bodies moved in sync, mirroring the unspoken harmony that existed between them.

In the quiet moments that followed, amidst the jazz club's ambiance, Alex and Sophia delved into conversations about their shared dreams and aspirations. They spoke of creating a life together that honored their individual passions while nurturing their love—a delicate balance they were determined to achieve.

As the night deepened, they wandered through the cobblestone streets of Greenwich Village, their hands intertwined, their hearts open. Under the moonlit sky, they shared hopes for the future, painting vivid pictures of the life they envisioned—a life filled with art, literature, and endless love.

Yet, amidst their harmonious moments, echoes of doubt resurfaced. Alex's art career faced new challenges, demanding more of his time and energy. Sophia's writing journey led her down unexpected paths, testing her resolve and dedication. The pressures of their individual pursuits threatened to disrupt the harmony they had found, but they refused to let it dim the brightness of their love.

A weekend retreat to a quaint bed-and-breakfast in upstate New York provided a much-needed escape from the city's frenetic pace. Surrounded by nature's tranquility, Alex and Sophia reconnected on a deeper level, reaffirming their commitment to each other and to their shared dreams.

As they sat by a cozy fireplace, their reflections illuminated by the warm glow, Alex and Sophia made a pact to navigate life's challenges together—to find harmony in the discord, to embrace the highs and lows with equal grace.

As the chapter drew to a close, a sense of unity pervaded their relationship—a recognition that in the symphony of life, their love was the melody that anchored them, guiding them through the ever-changing rhythms of New York City.

CHAPTER TEN
Dreams in the City's Canvas

As the vibrant colors of autumn painted the city's canvas, Alex and Sophia embarked on a journey of dreams intertwined—a tapestry woven with threads of love, passion, and unwavering determination. Their bond had weathered storms and danced through moments of serenity, but the true test lay in chasing their dreams while holding onto each other.

In a quaint art gallery nestled in Chelsea, Alex unveiled his latest collection—a symphony of colors and emotions that mirrored his journey through New York City. The gallery buzzed with excitement as art enthusiasts marveled at his creations, each stroke on canvas a reflection of his soul's whispers.

Amidst the admiration and accolades, Sophia stood by his side, her eyes filled with pride and love. She had witnessed Alex's artistic evolution, his struggles, and triumphs, and in that moment, she felt a deep sense of connection to his passion—a shared dream of creating a life filled with art, love, and endless possibilities.

As the evening unfolded, amidst the mingling of artists and patrons, Alex and Sophia found a quiet corner to reflect on their journey. They spoke of the dreams they had nurtured since the beginning—their desire to make a mark in the city's vibrant arts scene, to inspire others with their creativity, and to carve a path that echoed their love story.

Yet, amidst the celebration, shadows of doubt crept in. Alex faced the pressure to maintain his artistic integrity amidst commercial success, while Sophia grappled with the ever-present question of balancing her writing career with their shared aspirations.

A rooftop dinner overlooking the city skyline offered a moment of respite—a chance to pause amidst the chaos and bask in the beauty of their dreams taking shape. Under the starlit sky, with the city's lights shimmering below, Alex and Sophia made a pact to support each other's dreams unconditionally—to be each other's pillars of strength as they navigated the unpredictable terrain of their chosen paths.

As they raised a toast to love, art, and dreams fulfilled, a sense of purpose filled their hearts—a recognition that their journey was far from over, but with love as their compass, they were ready to paint their future on the canvas of New York City.

As the chapter drew to a close, a sense of anticipation lingered—an invitation to join Alex and Sophia as they chased their dreams with passion, determination, and a love that knew no bounds.

CHAPTER ELEVEN
Resonance in the City's Melody

As the winter chill settled over the city, Alex and Sophia found resonance in the harmonious melody of their love. The changing seasons mirrored the ebb and flow of their journey, with each moment bringing new challenges and opportunities for growth.

Amidst the holiday festivities adorning the city streets, Alex and Sophia sought refuge in familiar places that held memories of their journey together. They revisited the café where they had their first date, the park bench where they shared their hopes and fears, and the rooftop where they made promises of unwavering support.

In those moments of reflection, they realized how far they had come—the obstacles they had overcome, the dreams they had pursued, and the love that had remained constant through it all. They found solace in the familiarity of their shared history, knowing that every experience had shaped them into who they were now.

Yet, as the year drew to a close, a sense of uncertainty lingered. Alex's artistic pursuits faced new challenges, requiring him to push boundaries and explore uncharted territories. Sophia's writing journey took unexpected turns, leading her to question the direction of her career and the impact it had on their relationship.

A snowy evening in Central Park became a canvas for their introspection. Wrapped in layers of warmth and love, Alex and Sophia walked hand in hand, their footsteps leaving imprints in the pristine snow. They spoke of their hopes for the future, their fears of the unknown, and the dreams they still yearned to fulfill.

In a moment of vulnerability, Sophia voiced her concerns about the changes they were facing—the pressures of success, the sacrifices they had made, and the evolving dynamics of their relationship. Alex, in turn, shared his own apprehensions, acknowledging the complexities of balancing passion with practicality.

Amidst their shared uncertainties, they found strength in their shared love. They made a pact to face the challenges ahead together—to embrace the unknown with courage and resilience, knowing that their bond was the foundation upon which they could weather any storm.

As they watched the city sparkle with holiday lights, a sense of peace settled over them—a reassurance that no matter what the future held, their love would always be the guiding star in the city's vast expanse.

As the chapter drew to a close, a sense of anticipation lingered—an invitation to join Alex and Sophia as they embarked on a new chapter of their journey, navigating the complexities of life with love as their compass.

CHAPTER TWELVE
Illumination in the City's Shadows

As the city's lights cast long shadows in the winter evenings, Alex and Sophia found illumination in the depths of their bond. The contrast between light and shadow mirrored the complexities of their relationship, revealing hidden depths and newfound understanding.

Amidst the bustling holiday season, Alex and Sophia found themselves drawn to a photography exhibit showcasing the city's contrasts—the juxtaposition of light and shadow, chaos and calm. As they explored the gallery, they were struck by the profound beauty found in the interplay of opposites—a reflection of their own journey together.

In moments of quiet reflection, Alex and Sophia delved into conversations about the nuances of their relationship. They spoke of the highs and lows they had experienced, the lessons learned, and the growth that had come from facing challenges head-on. Each word spoken was a brushstroke on the canvas of their shared experiences, painting a picture of resilience and love.

Yet, amidst the holiday cheer, echoes of doubt lingered. Alex's artistic vision faced scrutiny from critics, testing his resolve and creativity. Sophia grappled with the expectations placed upon her as a writer, questioning whether she was living up to her potential.

A snowy evening stroll through Central Park became a metaphor for their journey. As they walked hand in hand, their breath forming misty clouds in the cold air, they embraced the beauty of imperfection. They found solace in the knowledge that their love was not defined by external validations but by the authenticity of their connection.

In a cozy café overlooking the city's skyline, Alex and Sophia shared their hopes for the future—a future filled with shared dreams, creative endeavors, and unwavering support. They made a pact to embrace both the light and shadow within themselves and each other—to find beauty in vulnerability and strength in acceptance.

As the holiday season drew to a close, a sense of clarity emerged—a recognition that their love was a beacon of light in the city's shadows, guiding them through life's uncertainties with courage and grace.

As the chapter concluded, a sense of anticipation lingered—an invitation to join Alex and Sophia as they continued to navigate the intricacies of their relationship, finding beauty and meaning in every moment shared in the city they called home.

CHAPTER THIRTEEN
Reflections in the City's Glow

As the winter nights grew longer, Alex and Sophia found themselves immersed in moments of reflection amidst the city's glow. The twinkling lights and bustling energy of New York provided the backdrop for their introspection, as they delved deeper into the intricacies of their relationship.

A visit to the Metropolitan Museum of Art sparked a conversation about the art of self-discovery. As they wandered through galleries filled with masterpieces, Alex and Sophia discussed the journey of understanding oneself within the context of their relationship. They explored themes of identity, growth, and the evolving dynamics that shaped their love story.

Back in their cozy apartment overlooking the city skyline, Alex and Sophia sat by the window, sipping hot cocoa as they gazed at the mesmerizing cityscape. They spoke of the reflections they saw in each other—the strengths, vulnerabilities, and the shared experiences that had brought them closer together.

Yet, amidst the warmth of their shared moments, challenges loomed on the horizon. Alex faced creative blocks, grappling with the pressure to innovate and stay true to his artistic vision. Sophia's writing journey took unexpected turns, leading her to question her place in the literary world and the impact of her words.

A spontaneous weekend getaway to a quaint cabin in the Catskill Mountains provided a much-needed escape from the city's hustle and bustle. Surrounded by nature's tranquility, Alex and Sophia found solace in the stillness, allowing them to delve deeper into their thoughts and emotions.

By a crackling fireplace, they opened up about their fears and aspirations, sharing their dreams for the future and the uncertainties that kept them awake at night. They acknowledged the challenges they faced individually and as a couple, finding comfort in the knowledge that they were not alone in their struggles.

As they ventured out for a moonlit walk in the snow-covered woods, Alex and Sophia found themselves lost in the beauty of nature's symphony. The crisp air and starlit sky seemed to echo the clarity they sought in their relationship—a reminder that even amidst uncertainty, there was beauty to be found in moments of stillness and connection.

As they returned to the city, refreshed and renewed, Alex and Sophia made a pact to embrace the journey of self-discovery together—to support each other's growth, celebrate their individuality, and find strength in their shared reflections.

As the chapter drew to a close, a sense of introspection lingered—an invitation to join Alex and Sophia as they continued to explore the depths of their love, finding beauty and meaning in the reflections of their journey.

CHAPTER FOURTEEN
Whispers of Change in the City's Rhythm

As the city's rhythm continued its steady beat, Alex and Sophia found themselves attuned to the whispers of change weaving through their lives. The new year brought with it a sense of anticipation and possibility, sparking conversations about the evolution of their dreams and aspirations.

A visit to a modern art exhibit in Chelsea sparked a dialogue about the nature of change and its impact on their relationship. Surrounded by avant-garde installations, Alex and Sophia explored the concept of embracing transformation while staying true to their core values and love for each other.

Back in their cozy apartment, they sat by the window overlooking the city's skyline, watching as snowflakes danced in the wintry breeze. They spoke of the changes they had witnessed in themselves and each other—the growth, the challenges overcome, and the dreams that had evolved along the way.

Yet, amidst the contemplation of change, uncertainties lingered. Alex's art career faced a turning point, presenting new opportunities that required him to step out of his comfort zone. Sophia's writing journey took unexpected twists, pushing her to explore new genres and storytelling techniques.

A weekend retreat to a rustic cabin by the Hudson River provided a space for reflection and renewal. Surrounded by nature's beauty, Alex and Sophia engaged in heartfelt conversations about their hopes for the future and the fears that held them back.

By a crackling fire, they shared their dreams of making a difference in the world through their art and words. They spoke of the challenges they anticipated, the risks they were willing to take, and the unwavering support they offered each other.

As they took a moonlit stroll along the riverbank, hand in hand, Alex and Sophia felt a sense of unity amidst the winds of change. The calm waters mirrored the serenity they found in each other's presence—a reminder that their love was a constant amidst life's uncertainties.

Back in the city, they made a pact to embrace change with open hearts—to welcome new opportunities, navigate challenges together, and continue growing both individually and as a couple.

As the chapter drew to a close, a sense of optimism filled the air—an invitation to join Alex and Sophia as they embraced the unfolding chapters of their lives, finding strength and resilience in the ever-changing rhythm of New York City.

CHAPTER FIFTEEN

Embracing Uncertainty in the City's Embrace

As the city's embrace held them close, Alex and Sophia found themselves at a crossroads of uncertainty and possibility. The changing seasons mirrored the shifting tides of their journey, inviting introspection and a deeper exploration of their dreams.

A visit to an art installation in the heart of SoHo sparked conversations about the beauty of impermanence. Surrounded by ephemeral works of art, Alex and Sophia pondered the transient nature of life and the importance of embracing change with open arms.

Back in their cozy apartment, they sat by the window, watching as raindrops painted patterns on the glass. The pitter-patter of rain against the city's streets became a metaphor for the rhythm of life—a reminder that amidst uncertainty, there was beauty to be found in the simplest moments.

Yet, amidst the contemplation of impermanence, doubts lingered. Alex faced decisions about the direction of his art—a path that held both excitement and fear of the unknown. Sophia's writing journey took unexpected turns, leading her to question her creative process and the impact of her words.

A spontaneous day trip to Coney Island provided a break from the city's hustle and bustle. As they strolled along the boardwalk, the salty sea breeze mingling with their thoughts, Alex and Sophia shared their hopes and fears for the future.

By the water's edge, they spoke of the uncertainties that lay ahead—the challenges they might face, the dreams they still wished to pursue, and the uncharted territories they were eager to explore together. In each other's presence, they found solace, knowing that they were not alone in navigating life's uncertainties.

As the sun set over the horizon, casting a golden glow on the beach, Alex and Sophia made a pact to embrace the unknown—to welcome change as a catalyst for growth, to find joy in the journey, and to cherish the moments of togetherness that anchored them amidst life's unpredictability.

Back in the city, amidst the bustling streets and towering skyscrapers, they carried with them a newfound sense of resilience and acceptance. They understood that uncertainty was not a barrier but a bridge—a bridge that led to new adventures, deeper connections, and the discovery of untapped potentials.

As the chapter drew to a close, a sense of peace settled over them—an invitation to join Alex and Sophia as they embraced the uncertainties of tomorrow with courage, love, and a willingness to let life unfold as it may in the city they called home.

CHAPTER SIXTEEN
Finding Clarity in the City's Chaos

Amidst the bustling chaos of the city, Alex and Sophia embarked on a journey of finding clarity amidst the noise and distractions. The urban landscape became a canvas for introspection, inviting them to delve deeper into their aspirations and dreams.

A chance encounter with a street artist in Washington Square Park sparked a conversation about the power of art to convey messages of clarity and truth. Surrounded by vibrant murals and expressive performances, Alex and Sophia discussed the importance of finding their own voices amidst the cacophony of life.

Back in their cozy apartment, they sat by a window overlooking the city's skyline, watching as the city lights flickered in the evening haze. The rhythm of the city below seemed to echo the rhythm of their thoughts—a symphony of ideas, hopes, and dreams waiting to be explored.

Yet, amidst the quest for clarity, doubts lingered. Alex grappled with the pressures of the art world, questioning whether his vision aligned with external expectations. Sophia's writing journey took twists and turns, leading her to confront her insecurities and fears of failure.

A weekend escape to the Brooklyn Botanic Garden provided a retreat from the city's hustle. Surrounded by nature's beauty, Alex and Sophia found moments of peace and clarity amidst the blooming flowers and tranquil ponds.

By a secluded bench, they shared their innermost thoughts and aspirations, finding comfort in the vulnerability of their conversations. They spoke of their dreams for the future, the challenges they faced, and the resilience that fueled their journey together.

As they wandered through the garden's winding paths, hand in hand, Alex and Sophia felt a sense of unity amidst the chaos of life. The serenity of the garden offered a respite from the uncertainties that plagued their minds, allowing them to focus on what truly mattered—their love and shared dreams.

Back in the city, they made a pact to embrace moments of clarity as they arose—to trust their instincts, follow their passions, and navigate the twists and turns of life with courage and determination.

As the chapter drew to a close, a sense of clarity settled over them—an invitation to join Alex and Sophia as they continued to seek clarity amidst the city's chaos, finding strength and purpose in their journey together.

CHAPTER SEVENTEEN
Navigating Storms in the City's Sky

As the city's sky darkened with approaching storms, Alex and Sophia found themselves navigating turbulent emotions and unforeseen challenges. The looming clouds mirrored the uncertainties that hovered over their relationship, testing their resilience and commitment to each other.

A visit to a rooftop bar in Midtown Manhattan brought them face to face with the city's changing weather—a metaphor for the shifts and upheavals they were experiencing. Surrounded by skyscrapers reaching for the sky, Alex and Sophia engaged in candid conversations about their fears, hopes, and the storms they faced together.

Back in their apartment, the sound of rain tapping against the windows added to the ambiance of introspection. They sat together, seeking solace in each other's presence as they discussed the challenges that had arisen in their respective pursuits.

Alex grappled with artistic blocks, unable to find inspiration amidst the chaos of his thoughts. Sophia's writing journey took unexpected detours, leading her to question her creative process and the impact of her words on their relationship.

A weekend retreat to a cozy cabin in the Catskill Mountains provided a much-needed escape from the city's intensity. Surrounded by nature's raw beauty, Alex and Sophia found moments of clarity amidst the stormy weather.

By a crackling fireplace, they opened up about their vulnerabilities and fears, finding comfort in sharing their struggles. They spoke of the pressures they faced, the doubts that clouded their minds, and the strength they drew from each other during challenging times.

As they ventured outside to explore the rugged terrain, the storm clouds gradually cleared, revealing patches of blue sky and rays of sunlight breaking through. Alex and Sophia took this as a metaphor for their own journey—acknowledging that storms were temporary and that clearer skies awaited on the other side.

Back in the city, they made a pact to weather the storms together—to support each other through the highs and lows, to find inspiration in moments of darkness, and to emerge stronger and more resilient as a couple.

As the chapter drew to a close, a sense of calm settled over them—an invitation to join Alex and Sophia as they navigated the storms of life, finding strength and unity amidst the ever-changing sky of New York City.

CHAPTER EIGHTEEN

Blooming Amidst the City's Concrete Jungle

As spring painted the city in vibrant hues, Alex and Sophia found themselves blooming amidst the concrete jungle of New York. The renewal of life and growth in nature mirrored the fresh beginnings and newfound clarity they embraced in their relationship.

A stroll through Central Park's Cherry Blossom Festival brought them in touch with the beauty of transformation. Surrounded by blossoming trees and a sea of pink petals, Alex and Sophia felt a sense of renewal wash over them—a reminder that growth often comes after the storms have passed.

Back in their apartment, they sat by an open window, letting in the fragrant breeze and the sounds of the city awakening to spring. The soft glow of sunlight filtering through the curtains illuminated their faces as they shared quiet moments of reflection.

Alex spoke of the creative sparks that had ignited within him, inspired by the beauty of the changing seasons. Sophia, too, found herself reinvigorated in her writing, channeling the essence of spring into her words.

Yet, amidst the newfound inspiration, challenges persisted. Alex faced the pressures of meeting deadlines and expectations in the art world, while Sophia grappled with self-doubt and the fear of not living up to her potential.

A weekend getaway to a botanical garden on the outskirts of the city provided a sanctuary for their souls. Surrounded by blooming flowers and lush greenery, Alex and Sophia found inspiration in the natural world's resilience and beauty.

By a tranquil pond, they engaged in conversations about their dreams and aspirations, allowing themselves to dream boldly and envision a future filled with possibilities. They spoke of their fears and uncertainties, but also of the courage and determination that fueled their journey forward.

As they wandered through the garden's winding paths, hand in hand, Alex and Sophia felt a sense of unity and purpose. The blossoming flowers seemed to echo their own growth—a testament to the beauty that could emerge from challenging times.

Back in the city, they made a pact to continue blooming together—to nurture their dreams, support each other's growth, and celebrate the milestones along the way.

As the chapter drew to a close, a sense of optimism filled the air—an invitation to join Alex and Sophia as they embraced the beauty of growth and renewal in the midst of the city's bustling energy.

CHAPTER NINETEEN
Harmony in the City's Symphony

As the city's symphony of life played on, Alex and Sophia found themselves in harmony amidst the bustling energy and vibrant rhythms of New York. The blend of sounds, colors, and experiences mirrored the depth and richness of their connection, weaving together a tapestry of love and shared experiences.

A visit to a jazz club in Harlem brought them closer to the heartbeat of the city's music scene. Surrounded by soulful melodies and rhythmic beats, Alex and Sophia felt a sense of unity in the power of music to transcend barriers and express emotions beyond words.

Back in their apartment, they sat together on the balcony, overlooking the city's skyline illuminated by the night's glow. The distant sounds of jazz clubs and bustling streets drifted through the air, creating a symphony of urban life that resonated with their own journey.

Alex spoke of the harmonies he found in his art, inspired by the diverse sounds and cultures of the city. Sophia, too, felt the melodies of her writing aligning with the rhythm of their shared experiences, weaving together stories of love and resilience.

Yet, amidst the harmonious moments, challenges continued to arise. Alex faced creative blocks, struggling to capture the essence of his artistic vision amidst external pressures. Sophia grappled with the complexities of balancing her writing career with their shared aspirations and dreams.

A weekend retreat to a serene lakeside cabin provided a peaceful escape from the city's frenetic pace. Surrounded by nature's tranquility, Alex and Sophia found solace in the quiet moments, allowing them to reconnect and rediscover the harmonies that bound them together.

By the water's edge, they engaged in heartfelt conversations about their passions, fears, and hopes for the future. They spoke of the challenges they faced individually and as a couple, but also of the strength they drew from their love and shared dreams.

As they gazed at the starlit sky reflected on the lake's surface, Alex and Sophia felt a sense of unity and alignment with the universe. The natural symphony of crickets and rustling leaves seemed to echo their own journey—a reminder that harmony could be found amidst life's complexities.

Back in the city, they made a pact to cultivate harmony in all aspects of their lives—to embrace the diverse melodies that made up their story, to navigate challenges with grace and resilience, and to celebrate the beauty of their harmonious connection.

As the chapter drew to a close, a sense of serenity settled over them—an invitation to join Alex and Sophia as they continued to dance to the city's symphony, finding harmony and joy in every note of their shared journey.

CHAPTER TWENTY
Resilience in the City's Heartbeat

Amidst the city's rhythmic heartbeat, Alex and Sophia discovered the strength of resilience weaving through the fabric of their lives. The pulse of the city echoed their own journey of overcoming challenges and finding resilience in the face of adversity.

A spontaneous visit to a spoken word poetry event in Brooklyn immersed them in the power of spoken words to inspire and heal. Surrounded by passionate performances and raw emotions, Alex and Sophia felt a renewed sense of courage and determination.

Back in their apartment, they sat together on the couch, sharing moments of vulnerability and strength. The city's sounds of traffic and distant sirens formed a backdrop to their conversations, a reminder of the constant motion and resilience required to thrive in urban life.

Alex spoke of the resilience he found in his art, using setbacks as stepping stones to greater creativity and expression. Sophia, too, reflected on her journey as a writer, drawing strength from the challenges she had faced and the lessons learned along the way.

Yet, amidst the resilience, doubts and uncertainties persisted. Alex faced rejection and criticism in the art world, testing his resolve and belief in his craft. Sophia grappled with self-doubt, questioning whether her words had the power to make a difference.

A weekend excursion to a historic landmark in the city provided a historical perspective on resilience. Surrounded by stories of triumph over adversity, Alex and Sophia found inspiration in the resilience of past generations, drawing parallels to their own journey.

By a monument symbolizing resilience, they engaged in conversations about resilience as a journey—a continuous process of growth, adaptation, and inner strength. They spoke of the challenges they faced individually and as a couple, but also of the resilience they had built together.

As they walked through the city streets, witnessing the hustle and bustle of everyday life, Alex and Sophia felt a sense of solidarity with the resilient spirit of the city. The diversity of people and experiences reminded them that resilience came in many forms, each contributing to the vibrant tapestry of urban life.

Back in their apartment, they made a pact to embrace resilience as a guiding force in their lives—to face challenges with courage, to learn from setbacks, and to celebrate the strength they found in each other's presence.

As the chapter drew to a close, a sense of determination filled the air—an invitation to join Alex and Sophia as they continued their journey of resilience, finding strength and inspiration in the city's heartbeat and their unwavering bond.

CHAPTER TWENTY-ONE
Connection in the City's Tapestry

In the intricate tapestry of the city, Alex and Sophia discovered the profound beauty of connection woven through every thread of their lives. The diverse experiences and people they encountered became threads that bound them together, creating a rich and vibrant tapestry of love and shared experiences.

A visit to a cultural festival in Little Italy immersed them in the rich heritage and traditions of different communities. Surrounded by vibrant colors, delicious aromas, and lively music, Alex and Sophia felt a deep sense of connection to the city's diverse tapestry of cultures.

Back in their apartment, they sat together, surrounded by mementos and souvenirs from their explorations. The city's sounds of languages and laughter from nearby streets formed a backdrop to their conversations, a reminder of the interconnectedness of humanity.

Alex spoke of the connections he felt in his art, drawing inspiration from the stories and experiences of people he met along the way. Sophia, too, reflected on the connections she forged through her writing, weaving together narratives that celebrated the human experience in all its diversity.

Yet, amidst the connections, challenges and complexities arose. Alex faced the pressures of balancing commercial success with artistic integrity, navigating the fine line between staying true to his vision and meeting market demands. Sophia grappled with the responsibility of representing diverse voices in her writing, striving to do justice to the stories she encountered.

A weekend gathering with friends from different backgrounds provided a space for meaningful connections. Surrounded by laughter and shared stories, Alex and Sophia found solace in the bonds of friendship and the joy of connecting with kindred spirits.

By a table filled with cultural delicacies, they engaged in conversations about the power of connection to bridge differences and foster understanding. They spoke of the challenges and rewards of building meaningful relationships, finding common ground amidst diverse perspectives.

As they walked through the city's neighborhoods, exploring hidden gems and cultural landmarks, Alex and Sophia felt a sense of belonging in the city's tapestry of stories and experiences. The diversity of voices and perspectives reminded them that connection was a shared human experience, transcending barriers of language, culture, and background.

Back in their apartment, they made a pact to cherish and nurture connections in all aspects of their lives—to embrace diversity, foster empathy, and celebrate the richness of human experience through meaningful relationships.

As the chapter drew to a close, a sense of warmth and unity filled the air—an invitation to join Alex and Sophia as they continued their journey of connection, finding beauty and inspiration in the city's vibrant tapestry of life and love.

CHAPTER TWENTY-TWO
Growth Amidst the City's Canvas

In the ever-evolving canvas of the city, Alex and Sophia discovered the beauty of growth woven through the layers of their journey. The city's vibrant energy and constant change became a backdrop for their own personal and creative growth, inspiring them to reach new heights.

A visit to an art exhibition in Chelsea showcased the diversity of artistic expression and innovation. Surrounded by captivating works of art, Alex and Sophia felt a surge of inspiration, recognizing the endless possibilities for growth and exploration in their own creative endeavors.

Back in their apartment, they sat amidst their own works in progress, surrounded by sketches, paintings, and manuscripts. The city's sounds of construction and bustling streets formed a symphony of progress, a reminder of the constant evolution and growth that defined urban life.

Alex spoke of the growth he had experienced in his art, experimenting with new techniques and pushing the boundaries of his creativity. Sophia, too, reflected on her journey of growth as a writer, embracing new genres and storytelling approaches that challenged and inspired her.

Yet, amidst the growth, challenges and uncertainties persisted. Alex faced the pressures of staying relevant in a rapidly changing art world, navigating trends and innovations while staying true to his artistic vision. Sophia grappled with self-doubt and imposter syndrome, questioning whether her words had the power to make a lasting impact.

A weekend retreat to a serene park in the city provided a space for introspection and renewal. Surrounded by nature's beauty, Alex and Sophia found moments of clarity amidst the chaos of their thoughts, allowing them to reflect on their personal and creative growth.

By a tranquil pond, they engaged in conversations about the journey of growth—a journey marked by challenges, setbacks, and moments of breakthrough. They spoke of the lessons they had learned along the way, the resilience they had built, and the dreams they still aspired to achieve.

As they walked through the park's winding paths, surrounded by blooming flowers and lush greenery, Alex and Sophia felt a sense of empowerment and possibility. The natural cycles of growth and renewal mirrored their own journey of evolution—a reminder that growth was a continuous process, fueled by passion and determination.

Back in their apartment, they made a pact to embrace growth in all aspects of their lives—to welcome challenges as opportunities for learning and growth, to push the boundaries of their creativity, and to never stop evolving as individuals and as a couple.

As the chapter drew to a close, a sense of excitement and anticipation filled the air—an invitation to join Alex and Sophia as they continued their journey of growth amidst the city's ever-changing canvas, finding inspiration and fulfillment in the endless possibilities that lay ahead.

CHAPTER TWENTY-THREE
Reflections in the City's Mirrors

In the reflective surfaces of the city's mirrors, Alex and Sophia discovered the power of introspection and self-discovery. The urban landscape became a metaphor for their own journey of looking within, confronting truths, and finding clarity amidst the complexities of life.

A visit to an art installation in Lower Manhattan, featuring interactive mirrors that reflected visitors' images in unique ways, sparked introspective conversations. Surrounded by mirrored surfaces that distorted and transformed their reflections, Alex and Sophia delved into discussions about identity, perception, and self-awareness.

Back in their apartment, they sat in front of a large mirror, exploring their own reflections and the stories they told. The city's sounds of traffic and distant chatter filtered through the windows, adding to the reflective ambiance of the moment.

Alex spoke of the self-discovery he had experienced through his art, using his creations as a mirror to explore his emotions and innermost thoughts. Sophia, too, reflected on her journey of self-discovery as a writer, delving into themes of identity and personal growth in her narratives.

Yet, amidst the reflections, challenges and insecurities arose. Alex grappled with self-doubt, questioning his place in the art world and the impact of his work. Sophia faced inner conflicts about authenticity and vulnerability in her writing, wondering how much of herself to reveal on the page.

A weekend getaway to a tranquil lake in upstate New York provided a space for quiet reflection. Surrounded by nature's serenity, Alex and Sophia found moments of introspection amidst the stillness, allowing them to confront their fears and uncertainties.

By the water's edge, they engaged in conversations about the mirrors of life—a metaphor for the roles, masks, and perceptions that shaped their identities. They spoke of the importance of self-awareness, acceptance, and embracing authenticity in their creative endeavors and personal lives.

As they sat beneath a starry sky, reflecting on the journey of self-discovery, Alex and Sophia felt a sense of liberation and empowerment. The vastness of the night sky mirrored the infinite possibilities for growth and transformation that lay within each of them.

Back in their apartment, they made a pact to embrace their reflections—to confront their shadows, celebrate their strengths, and continue the journey of self-discovery with courage and compassion.

As the chapter drew to a close, a sense of clarity and understanding filled the air—an invitation to join Alex and Sophia as they explored the mirrors of their souls, finding beauty and truth in the reflections of their shared journey.

CHAPTER TWENTY-FOUR
Illumination in the City's Shadows

Amidst the city's shadows, Alex and Sophia discovered the power of illumination—the ability to find light and clarity even in the darkest moments. The contrast of light and shadow became a metaphor for their journey of facing challenges, confronting fears, and finding inner strength.

A visit to an art exhibit showcasing light installations in a gallery in SoHo sparked conversations about the interplay of light and darkness in life. Surrounded by mesmerizing light sculptures that transformed the space, Alex and Sophia explored themes of resilience, hope, and the human spirit's ability to shine through adversity.

Back in their apartment, they sat by a window overlooking the city's skyline as night fell, casting shadows and highlighting the city's illuminated landmarks. The sounds of the city at night—the hum of traffic, distant sirens, and occasional laughter—formed a backdrop to their discussions about finding light in life's shadows.

Alex spoke of the moments of illumination he had experienced in his art, using light as a metaphor for hope and inspiration in his creations. Sophia, too, reflected on her journey of finding light in her writing, exploring themes of resilience and redemption in her stories.

Yet, amidst the illumination, challenges and doubts persisted. Alex faced creative blocks and self-criticism, grappling with the pressure to constantly innovate and create meaningful work. Sophia navigated personal insecurities and fears, questioning her ability to find light in the midst of life's challenges.

A weekend retreat to a lighthouse on the coast provided a symbolic space for reflection and introspection. Surrounded by the beacon of light that guided ships safely through the darkness, Alex and Sophia found moments of clarity amidst the solitude, allowing them to confront their shadows and fears.

By the lighthouse's glow, they engaged in conversations about illumination—a metaphor for finding hope, purpose, and inner peace in life's journey. They spoke of the lessons learned from navigating darkness, the resilience gained from facing challenges, and the transformative power of finding light within oneself.

As they stood on the lighthouse balcony, gazing at the stars and the vast expanse of the ocean, Alex and Sophia felt a sense of awe and wonder. The lighthouse's beam of light cutting through the night mirrored their own journey of illumination—a reminder that even in the darkest moments, there was always a glimmer of hope and possibility.

Back in their apartment, they made a pact to seek illumination in all aspects of their lives—to embrace challenges as opportunities for growth, to find inspiration in moments of darkness, and to shine their light brightly in the world.

As the chapter drew to a close, a sense of resilience and optimism filled the air—an invitation to join Alex and Sophia as they continued their journey of illumination, finding strength and beauty in the city's shadows and the light they carried within.

CHAPTER TWENTY-FIVE
Harmony Amidst the City's Chaos

In the midst of the city's chaos, Alex and Sophia discovered the beauty of harmony—a symphony of balance and unity that transcended the noise and distractions of urban life. The contrasts of chaos and harmony became a metaphor for their journey of finding peace, balance, and connection amidst the bustling energy of the city.

A visit to a meditation retreat in the heart of Manhattan provided a sanctuary from the city's noise. Surrounded by serene gardens and tranquil spaces, Alex and Sophia delved into practices of mindfulness and inner stillness, finding moments of peace amidst the chaos of their minds.

Back in their apartment, they created a meditation corner—a sacred space filled with candles, incense, and calming music. The city's sounds of traffic and distant conversations formed a backdrop to their meditation sessions, a reminder of the constant ebb and flow of life's rhythms.

Alex spoke of the harmony he found in moments of stillness, using meditation as a tool to quiet the mind and connect with a deeper sense of self. Sophia, too, reflected on her journey of finding inner peace, exploring themes of mindfulness and presence in her writing.

Yet, amidst the harmony, challenges and distractions persisted. Alex faced the pressures of productivity and external expectations, struggling to find balance amidst a busy schedule. Sophia grappled with the distractions of modern life, finding it challenging to stay present and focused on her creative endeavors.

A weekend retreat to a nature reserve on the outskirts of the city provided a grounding experience in the midst of chaos. Surrounded by towering trees and the sounds of birdsong, Alex and Sophia found solace in the simplicity of nature, allowing them to reconnect with their inner harmony.

By a peaceful stream, they engaged in conversations about harmony—a delicate balance of mind, body, and spirit that required nurturing and mindfulness. They spoke of the challenges of finding inner peace in a world filled with distractions, but also of the rewards of moments of stillness and presence.

As they walked through the forest's winding paths, feeling the earth beneath their feet and the breeze on their skin, Alex and Sophia felt a sense of unity with nature's rhythms. The harmony of the natural world mirrored their own journey of finding balance amidst life's chaos.

Back in their apartment, they made a pact to cultivate harmony in all aspects of their lives—to prioritize moments of stillness and self-care, to set boundaries with external distractions, and to embrace the beauty of balance in their daily routines.

As the chapter drew to a close, a sense of calm and serenity filled the air—an invitation to join Alex and Sophia as they continued their journey of harmony, finding peace and unity amidst the city's bustling chaos and the harmonious melodies they created within.

CHAPTER TWENTY-SIX
Discovery in the City's Labyrinths

Amidst the city's labyrinths of streets and alleys, Alex and Sophia embarked on a journey of discovery—a quest to uncover hidden truths, explore new horizons, and embrace the unknown. The maze-like urban landscape became a metaphor for their adventure of self-discovery and exploration.

A visit to an art installation in a hidden underground gallery sparked their curiosity. Surrounded by avant-garde sculptures and immersive installations, Alex and Sophia delved into discussions about the layers of meaning hidden beneath the surface, drawing parallels to their own quest for deeper understanding.

Back in their apartment, they surrounded themselves with maps, books, and artifacts from different cultures—a tribute to their shared love for exploration and discovery. The city's sounds of footsteps echoing in narrow alleyways and distant sirens formed a backdrop to their conversations about the mysteries and wonders waiting to be uncovered.

Alex spoke of the discoveries he made in his art, exploring new techniques and themes that challenged and inspired him. Sophia, too, reflected on her journey of discovery as a writer, venturing into uncharted territories of storytelling and imagination.

Yet, amidst the discoveries, challenges and uncertainties persisted. Alex faced creative blocks and self-doubt, questioning whether he had explored all avenues of artistic expression. Sophia grappled with the fear of the unknown, unsure of what lay ahead in her writing journey.

A weekend exploration of the city's hidden gems and secret spots provided a thrilling adventure of discovery. From hidden rooftop gardens to underground speakeasies, Alex and Sophia immersed themselves in the city's secrets, uncovering stories and experiences that sparked their imagination.

By a hidden mural in a forgotten alley, they engaged in conversations about discovery—a journey of curiosity, courage, and open-mindedness. They spoke of the importance of stepping out of comfort zones, embracing challenges, and welcoming the unexpected twists and turns of life.

As they navigated the city's labyrinthine streets, getting lost and found in equal measure, Alex and Sophia felt a sense of liberation and excitement. The maze of possibilities mirrored their own journey of self-discovery—a reminder that every twist and turn held the potential for growth and revelation.

Back in their apartment, they made a pact to embrace discovery in all its forms—to remain curious, to seek out new experiences, and to welcome the unknown with open arms and hearts.

As the chapter drew to a close, a sense of adventure and anticipation filled the air—an invitation to join Alex and Sophia as they continued their journey of discovery, navigating the city's labyrinths and unraveling the mysteries of their own hearts and minds.

CHAPTER TWENTY-SEVEN
Connection in the City's Melodies

Amidst the city's melodies, Alex and Sophia discovered the power of connection through music—a universal language that transcended barriers and brought people together. The symphony of sounds in the urban landscape became a backdrop for their exploration of harmony, unity, and shared experiences.

A visit to a jazz club in Greenwich Village immersed them in the soulful rhythms and improvisations of live music. Surrounded by the energy of musicians and fellow music enthusiasts, Alex and Sophia felt a deep sense of connection to the city's musical heartbeat, a reminder of the power of music to evoke emotions and forge bonds.

Back in their apartment, they curated playlists of their favorite songs and genres—a soundtrack that reflected the diversity of their musical tastes and shared memories. The city's sounds of street performers and distant concerts formed a backdrop to their conversations about the role of music in their lives and relationships.

Alex spoke of the connections he felt through music, using melodies and lyrics as a way to express emotions and connect with others. Sophia, too, reflected on her journey of musical discovery, finding solace and inspiration in melodies that resonated with her soul.

Yet, amidst the musical connections, challenges and obstacles persisted. Alex faced the pressures of staying authentic in his music, navigating the demands of the industry while staying true to his artistic vision. Sophia grappled with self-doubt and stage fright, unsure of her musical abilities and potential.

A weekend excursion to a music festival in the city provided a vibrant celebration of musical diversity. From classical orchestras to indie bands, Alex and Sophia immersed themselves in a tapestry of musical genres, finding common ground and new inspirations in the melodies that filled the air.

By a riverbank stage, they engaged in conversations about the power of music to unite people from different backgrounds and cultures. They spoke of the universal language of melodies, the emotions they evoked, and the connections they fostered between individuals and communities.

As they danced under the starlit sky, surrounded by fellow music lovers, Alex and Sophia felt a sense of unity and belonging. The harmonies and rhythms of the music mirrored their own journey of connection—a reminder that music had the power to heal, inspire, and unite.

Back in their apartment, they made a pact to keep music at the heart of their relationship—to share moments of joy and introspection through songs, to support each other's musical aspirations, and to let the melodies guide them on their shared journey.

As the chapter drew to a close, a sense of harmony and togetherness filled the air—an invitation to join Alex and Sophia as they continued their musical journey, finding connection and joy in the city's vibrant melodies and the harmonies they created together.

CHAPTER TWENTY-EIGHT
Resilience in the City's Storms

Amidst the city's storms, Alex and Sophia discovered the strength of resilience—a steadfast determination to weather life's challenges and emerge stronger on the other side. The tumultuous weather patterns of the urban landscape became a metaphor for their own journey of facing adversity, finding inner strength, and embracing growth.

A sudden summer storm caught them by surprise as they walked through the city streets. The rain poured down in torrents, thunder echoing through the skyscrapers, and lightning illuminating the darkened sky. Seeking shelter in a nearby café, Alex and Sophia found themselves in the midst of a literal and metaphorical storm.

As they sipped hot beverages and watched the rain cascade down the windows, they delved into conversations about resilience—a quality they had both cultivated through life's challenges. Alex spoke of the resilience he had developed in his artistic journey, overcoming setbacks and rejection to continue pursuing his passion. Sophia, too, reflected on her journey of resilience as a writer, navigating moments of doubt and uncertainty to keep moving forward.

Yet, amidst the storm, challenges and obstacles persisted. Alex faced creative blocks and financial pressures, grappling with the unpredictable nature of the art world. Sophia grappled with personal setbacks and health issues, learning to prioritize self-care and resilience in the face of adversity.

A weekend retreat to a coastal town during a stormy season provided a powerful metaphor for resilience. Surrounded by crashing waves and howling winds, Alex and Sophia witnessed the raw power of nature, a reminder of the resilience required to withstand life's storms.

By the shoreline, they engaged in conversations about resilience—a journey marked by perseverance, adaptability, and strength in the face of adversity. They spoke of the lessons learned from weathering past storms, the growth that came from overcoming challenges, and the resilience they had built together as a couple.

As they stood on the beach, watching the stormy sea and feeling the wind whip around them, Alex and Sophia felt a sense of empowerment and resilience. The chaos of the storm mirrored their own journey of resilience—a reminder that challenges were opportunities for growth and transformation.

Back in their apartment, they made a pact to embrace resilience in all aspects of their lives—to face challenges with courage, to adapt to changing circumstances, and to find strength in moments of adversity.

As the chapter drew to a close, a sense of empowerment and determination filled the air—an invitation to join Alex and Sophia as they continued their journey of resilience, finding strength and growth in the city's storms and the resilience they embodied within.

CHAPTER TWENTY-NINE
Growth Amidst the City's Gardens

Amidst the city's gardens, Alex and Sophia discovered the beauty of growth—a continuous process of renewal, transformation, and blooming potential. The lush greenery and vibrant blooms of urban parks became a metaphor for their own journey of personal and creative growth.

A visit to a botanical garden in the heart of the city immersed them in a world of flora and fauna. Surrounded by exotic plants and fragrant flowers, Alex and Sophia marveled at nature's resilience and the cycle of growth and renewal that unfolded before them.

As they walked along winding paths, surrounded by colorful blooms and the soothing sounds of birdsong, they engaged in conversations about growth—a journey of self-discovery, learning, and embracing change. Alex spoke of the growth he had experienced in his art, experimenting with new techniques and pushing the boundaries of his creativity. Sophia, too, reflected on her journey of personal growth, exploring themes of resilience and self-expression in her writing.

Yet, amidst the beauty of growth, challenges and uncertainties persisted. Alex faced moments of self-doubt and artistic blocks, questioning his ability to evolve as an artist. Sophia grappled with fears of stagnation and complacency, seeking new ways to nurture her creativity and personal growth.

A weekend retreat to a botanical sanctuary outside the city provided a deeper immersion into the world of growth. Surrounded by towering trees and vibrant blooms, Alex and Sophia found inspiration in nature's ability to thrive and adapt, despite changing seasons and external pressures.

By a tranquil pond, they engaged in conversations about growth—a journey marked by resilience, curiosity, and a willingness to embrace new beginnings. They spoke of the lessons learned from facing challenges, the joys of self-discovery, and the transformative power of growth in their lives and relationship.

As they sat beneath a canopy of trees, feeling the earth beneath their feet and the sun's warmth on their skin, Alex and Sophia felt a sense of renewal and possibility. The beauty of the garden mirrored their own journey of growth—a reminder that every experience, whether joyful or challenging, contributed to their growth and evolution.

Back in their apartment, they made a pact to embrace growth in all aspects of their lives—to welcome change, to seek new opportunities for learning and self-improvement, and to nurture their dreams and aspirations with courage and determination.

As the chapter drew to a close, a sense of optimism and renewal filled the air—an invitation to join Alex and Sophia as they continued their journey of growth, finding beauty and potential in the city's gardens and the growth they fostered within themselves.

CHAPTER THIRTY
Reflections in the City's Mirrors

In the city's bustling streets, Alex and Sophia encountered reflections of themselves—moments of introspection and self-discovery that would shape their journey in unexpected ways. The mirrors scattered throughout the urban landscape became a metaphor for their inner reflections, prompting them to confront their truths, aspirations, and the complexities of their relationship.

A chance encounter with an art installation featuring mirrored mosaics in a downtown gallery sparked a journey of reflection for Alex and Sophia. Surrounded by fragmented reflections and shifting perspectives, they delved into conversations about self-awareness, identity, and the nuances of their connection.

As they stood before a mirrored wall, seeing themselves reflected in countless fragments, they engaged in discussions about the layers of their personalities, dreams, and fears. Alex spoke of the reflections he saw in his art—a mirror of emotions, experiences, and aspirations woven into his creations. Sophia, too, reflected on her journey of self-discovery, exploring themes of identity and purpose in her writing.

Yet, amidst the reflections, challenges and tensions persisted. Alex grappled with questions about his artistic identity and the direction of his work, feeling torn between commercial success and artistic integrity. Sophia faced moments of doubt and insecurity, questioning her role in their relationship and the impact of their long-distance dynamic.

A weekend retreat to a mirrored maze installation in an art park provided a surreal backdrop for introspection. Surrounded by endless reflections and twisting corridors, Alex and Sophia navigated the maze of their thoughts and emotions, seeking clarity and understanding.

By a central reflecting pool, they engaged in conversations about self-reflection—a journey of introspection, growth, and acceptance. They spoke of the mirrors they faced within themselves, the truths they uncovered, and the challenges of navigating personal and creative identities in a world of complexities.

As they walked through the maze, seeing themselves reflected from different angles and perspectives, Alex and Sophia felt a sense of clarity and insight. The mirrors became a catalyst for self-discovery—a reminder that true growth and understanding often required facing one's reflections and embracing the complexities within.

Back in their apartment, they made a pact to continue their journey of self-reflection—to embrace vulnerability, to confront their truths with honesty and compassion, and to nurture their relationship with openness and understanding.

As the chapter drew to a close, a sense of introspection and renewal filled the air—an invitation to join Alex and Sophia as they continued their journey of self-discovery, finding wisdom and insights in the city's mirrors and the reflections they encountered within.

CHAPTER THIRTY-ONE
Harmony in the City's Symphony

Amidst the city's symphony of sounds, Alex and Sophia discovered the beauty of harmony—a delicate balance of melodies, rhythms, and emotions that echoed their own journey of finding unity and connection. The cacophony of urban noises and musical compositions became a metaphor for their evolving relationship and the harmonies they sought to create together.

A spontaneous visit to a street performance by a local orchestra in Central Park brought Alex and Sophia into the heart of the city's musical landscape. Surrounded by the rich tones of violins, cellos, and brass instruments, they marveled at the harmony created by musicians from diverse backgrounds, each contributing their unique voice to the collective symphony.

As they sat on a blanket beneath the stars, listening to the music blend seamlessly with the city's ambient sounds, they engaged in conversations about harmony—a journey of understanding, collaboration, and mutual respect. Alex spoke of the harmonies he found in his art, weaving together colors, shapes, and emotions to create a cohesive narrative. Sophia, too, reflected on her quest for harmony in their relationship, navigating differences and finding common ground amidst the challenges of distance and individual pursuits.

Yet, amidst the harmonies, tensions and conflicts persisted. Alex grappled with feelings of inadequacy and comparison, struggling to find his place in the competitive art scene. Sophia faced moments of insecurity and jealousy, questioning her role in Alex's life and the impact of their separate paths on their connection.

A weekend getaway to a music retreat in upstate New York provided a transformative experience in the pursuit of harmony. Surrounded by fellow musicians and mentors, Alex and Sophia immersed themselves in workshops and performances, learning the art of collaborative harmony and the power of unified expression.

By a lakeside bonfire, they engaged in conversations about musical harmony—a synergy of individual talents, trust, and shared vision. They spoke of the challenges of finding balance and unity, the rewards of collaboration, and the joy of creating something greater than themselves through harmonious cooperation.

As they played music together, their instruments blending in perfect synchronization, Alex and Sophia felt a sense of connection and unity. The harmonies they created mirrored their own journey of finding harmony in their relationship—a reminder that true harmony required understanding, communication, and a willingness to listen and adapt.

Back in their apartment, they made a pact to prioritize harmony in their interactions—to communicate openly, to resolve conflicts with empathy, and to celebrate the beauty of their differences as complementary notes in the symphony of their love.

As the chapter drew to a close, a sense of peace and unity filled the air—an invitation to join Alex and Sophia as they continued their journey of harmony, finding solace and joy in the city's symphony and the harmonies they created together.

CHAPTER THIRTY-TWO
Shadows in the City's Lights

Amidst the city's vibrant lights, Alex and Sophia encountered shadows—moments of darkness and introspection that cast new perspectives on their journey. The interplay of light and shadow in the urban landscape became a metaphor for the complexities of their relationship, where moments of illumination were often accompanied by shadows of doubt and uncertainty.

A nighttime stroll through Times Square immersed Alex and Sophia in a dazzling display of lights and colors. Neon signs, billboards, and the glow of street lamps created a surreal backdrop, highlighting the contrasts between brightness and shadowy corners.

As they walked hand in hand, soaking in the electric atmosphere of the city at night, they engaged in conversations about shadows—a journey of exploring hidden depths, facing fears, and embracing vulnerability. Alex spoke of the shadows he encountered in his art, using contrasts and shades to evoke depth and emotion in his creations. Sophia, too, reflected on her experience of shadows in their relationship, navigating moments of insecurity and fear of the unknown.

Yet, amidst the shadows, moments of clarity and insight emerged. Alex confronted his fears of failure and rejection, recognizing that the shadows in his artistic journey were integral to growth and learning. Sophia acknowledged her own shadows of self-doubt, finding strength in vulnerability and open communication with Alex.

A weekend retreat to a dimly lit art gallery in the city provided a contemplative space to explore the shadows within. Surrounded by evocative artworks that played with light and darkness, Alex and Sophia delved into discussions about the beauty and complexity of shadows—a reflection of life's contrasts and paradoxes.

By a dimly lit sculpture, they engaged in conversations about embracing shadows—a journey of self-acceptance, resilience, and finding beauty in imperfection. They spoke of the shadows they saw in each other, the fears and insecurities that shaped their interactions, and the courage it took to confront and embrace those shadows together.

As they stood in the gallery, surrounded by shifting shadows and nuanced artworks, Alex and Sophia felt a sense of acceptance and understanding. The interplay of light and darkness mirrored their own journey of navigating highs and lows, moments of clarity and confusion, and the constant dance between illumination and shadows in their relationship.

Back in their apartment, they made a pact to embrace the shadows as part of their journey—to acknowledge the complexities and challenges, to learn from moments of darkness, and to find strength and resilience in facing the shadows together.

As the chapter drew to a close, a sense of acceptance and growth filled the air—an invitation to join Alex and Sophia as they continued their journey of exploration, finding beauty and wisdom in the city's lights and shadows, and the shadows they embraced within themselves and each other.

CHAPTER THIRTY-THREE
Echoes in the City's Silence

In the city's moments of silence, Alex and Sophia discovered echoes—resonances of past experiences, unspoken emotions, and untold stories that reverberated through their journey. The quiet moments amidst the urban buzz became a canvas for introspection, reflection, and the discovery of hidden truths.

A late-night walk along the High Line park offered Alex and Sophia a reprieve from the city's constant motion. Surrounded by the hushed tones of nature and distant traffic, they found themselves immersed in the echoes of their own thoughts and emotions.

As they strolled along the elevated park, overlooking the city's skyline, they engaged in conversations about echoes—a journey of listening, understanding, and uncovering layers of meaning. Alex spoke of the echoes he felt in his art, using symbolism and metaphor to convey the depths of human experience. Sophia, too, reflected on the echoes in their relationship, exploring moments of resonance and significance that shaped their connection.

Yet, amidst the echoes, unresolved emotions and unspoken truths lingered. Alex grappled with unexpressed feelings and the weight of past experiences that colored his perceptions. Sophia faced moments of introspection and self-discovery, seeking clarity in the echoes of their shared memories.

A weekend retreat to a quiet cabin in the outskirts of the city provided a serene backdrop for exploring echoes. Surrounded by the sounds of nature and the absence of city noise, Alex and Sophia delved into discussions about the power of echoes—a reflection of the past, a guide for the present, and a source of wisdom for the future.

By a crackling fireplace, they engaged in conversations about listening to echoes—a journey of empathy, forgiveness, and healing. They spoke of the echoes they heard in each other's words and actions, the resonance of shared experiences, and the importance of acknowledging and addressing unresolved echoes in their relationship.

As they sat in the quiet cabin, surrounded by the echoes of their shared laughter and whispered conversations, Alex and Sophia felt a sense of connection and understanding. The echoes became a bridge between past and present—a reminder of the richness of their journey together and the potential for growth and transformation.

Back in their apartment, they made a pact to listen to the echoes with open hearts—to honor the resonance of their shared experiences, to address unresolved emotions and conflicts, and to embrace the echoes as a source of guidance and insight.

As the chapter drew to a close, a sense of peace and clarity filled the air—an invitation to join Alex and Sophia as they continued their journey of listening to echoes, finding meaning and understanding in the city's moments of silence, and the echoes they embraced within themselves and each other.

CHAPTER THIRTY-FOUR
Whispers in the City's Winds

In the city's gentle winds, Alex and Sophia discovered whispers—subtle messages of hope, encouragement, and guidance that carried them through moments of uncertainty and doubt. The soft breezes that swept through the urban landscape became a conduit for whispers of wisdom, love, and resilience.

A stroll along the Brooklyn waterfront at dusk brought Alex and Sophia into the embrace of the city's winds. As they watched the sun set over the skyline, they felt the whispers of the wind brushing against their skin, carrying with them a sense of peace and tranquility.

As they walked hand in hand, enveloped in the gentle caress of the breeze, they engaged in conversations about whispers—a journey of intuition, faith, and the power of subtle messages. Alex spoke of the whispers he heard in his art, subtle nuances and hidden meanings that added depth to his creations. Sophia, too, reflected on the whispers in their relationship, moments of intuition and insight that guided their decisions and actions.

Yet, amidst the whispers, doubts and insecurities lingered. Alex grappled with uncertainties about his artistic path and the challenges of staying true to his vision. Sophia faced moments of self-doubt and fear of the unknown, seeking reassurance in the whispers of their shared dreams.

A weekend retreat to a quiet lighthouse on the outskirts of the city provided a sanctuary for exploring whispers. Surrounded by the sound of crashing waves and the rustle of wind through the grass, Alex and Sophia delved into discussions about the power of whispers—a source of guidance, comfort, and inspiration.

By a cliff overlooking the ocean, they engaged in conversations about listening to whispers—a journey of trust, intuition, and inner wisdom. They spoke of the whispers they felt in their hearts and souls, the gentle nudges that guided their choices and beliefs, and the importance of tuning into the whispers of their relationship.

As they stood in the quiet solitude of the lighthouse, feeling the whispers of the wind enveloping them, Alex and Sophia felt a sense of connection and clarity. The whispers became a source of strength and guidance—a reminder that even in moments of uncertainty, they could trust in the whispers of their hearts and the wisdom of their shared journey.

Back in their apartment, they made a pact to listen to the whispers with open minds—to embrace the subtle messages of hope and guidance, to trust in their intuition and inner wisdom, and to let the whispers of love and resilience carry them forward.

As the chapter drew to a close, a sense of serenity and purpose filled the air—an invitation to join Alex and Sophia as they continued their journey of listening to whispers, finding solace and inspiration in the city's winds, and the whispers of love and guidance they cherished within themselves and each other.

CHAPTER THIRTY-FIVE
Dance in the City's Rain

In the city's gentle rain, Alex and Sophia discovered the beauty of dance—a rhythmic expression of joy, passion, and connection that mirrored their own journey of embracing life's unpredictable moments. The soft patter of raindrops against the pavement became a symphony for their hearts, inviting them to dance in the rhythm of the city's embrace.

A sudden downpour caught Alex and Sophia by surprise as they walked through Central Park. With laughter and excitement, they embraced the rain, letting it wash over them like a cleansing wave. As they danced together amidst the droplets, they felt a sense of freedom and exhilaration, their movements syncing with the rhythm of nature.

As they twirled and spun in the rain-soaked park, they engaged in conversations about dance—a journey of spontaneity, expression, and letting go. Alex spoke of the dance he found in his art, using brushstrokes and colors to convey movement and emotion. Sophia, too, reflected on the dance in their relationship, moments of connection and harmony that transcended words.

Yet, amidst the dance, challenges and obstacles persisted. Alex grappled with doubts about his artistic direction and the pressures of external expectations. Sophia faced moments of uncertainty and fear of vulnerability, seeking reassurance in the dance of their shared experiences.

A weekend retreat to a lively dance studio in the heart of the city provided a vibrant backdrop for exploring the beauty of dance. Surrounded by music and fellow dancers, Alex and Sophia immersed themselves in workshops and performances, letting the rhythm guide their movements and emotions.

By a mirrored wall, they engaged in conversations about dancing through life—a journey of resilience, creativity, and connection. They spoke of the dance they shared in their hearts and souls, the synchronicity of their dreams and aspirations, and the importance of embracing spontaneity and joy in their relationship.

As they danced together, their bodies moving in harmony with the music, Alex and Sophia felt a sense of unity and freedom. The dance became a celebration of their journey—a reminder that even in moments of doubt and challenge, they could find solace and strength in the rhythm of their love.

Back in their apartment, they made a pact to dance through life with open hearts—to embrace the beauty of spontaneity and joy, to trust in the rhythm of their connection, and to let the dance of their love guide them through every step.

As the chapter drew to a close, a sense of exhilaration and unity filled the air—an invitation to join Alex and Sophia as they continued their journey of dancing in the rain, finding beauty and grace in life's unpredictable moments, and the dance of love they shared within themselves and each other.

CHAPTER THIRTY-SIX
Solitude in the City's Sanctuary

In the city's hidden sanctuaries, Alex and Sophia discovered the power of solitude—a tranquil refuge amidst the chaos of urban life where they could find inner peace, clarity, and renewal. The quiet corners and serene spaces became a haven for introspection, contemplation, and the exploration of inner landscapes.

A visit to a secluded botanical garden tucked away in the heart of the city offered Alex and Sophia a sanctuary of greenery and serenity. Surrounded by lush foliage and the soothing sounds of nature, they felt a sense of calm wash over them, easing the stresses of daily life.

As they wandered through winding paths and peaceful gardens, they engaged in conversations about solitude—a journey of self-discovery, reflection, and reconnecting with inner truths. Alex spoke of the solitude he found in his art, moments of focused creativity and introspection that allowed him to channel his emotions and visions. Sophia, too, reflected on the solitude in their relationship, moments of quiet understanding and connection that deepened their bond.

Yet, amidst the solitude, echoes of past challenges and unanswered questions lingered. Alex grappled with lingering doubts about his artistic path and the search for validation and recognition. Sophia faced moments of introspection and self-exploration, seeking clarity in the quiet moments of solitude.

A weekend retreat to a remote cabin nestled in the woods outside the city provided an immersive experience in the power of solitude. Surrounded by towering trees and the gentle sounds of nature, Alex and Sophia embraced the opportunity for deep introspection and connection with their inner selves.

By a tranquil stream, they engaged in conversations about embracing solitude—a journey of inner peace, acceptance, and self-discovery. They spoke of the solitude they found within themselves, the insights and revelations that emerged in moments of quiet reflection, and the importance of honoring their individual journeys while nurturing their shared path.

As they sat by the stream, listening to the soothing sounds of flowing water, Alex and Sophia felt a sense of unity and understanding. The solitude became a bridge between past and present—a reminder that true connection and growth often required moments of introspection and self-awareness.

Back in their apartment, they made a pact to embrace solitude as a source of strength and clarity—to carve out moments of quiet reflection, to honor their individual paths, and to support each other in their journeys of self-discovery.

As the chapter drew to a close, a sense of serenity and renewal filled the air—an invitation to join Alex and Sophia as they continued their journey of solitude, finding sanctuary and wisdom in the city's hidden oases, and the solitude they cherished within themselves and each other.

CHAPTER THIRTY-SEVEN
Harmony in the City's Melodies

In the city's vibrant melodies, Alex and Sophia discovered the power of harmony—a symphonic blend of their individual voices, dreams, and aspirations that created a beautiful tapestry of shared experiences. The music that filled the urban spaces became a soundtrack for their journey, weaving together moments of joy, passion, and connection.

A visit to a bustling music festival in the heart of the city immersed Alex and Sophia in a symphony of sounds and rhythms. Surrounded by live performances and diverse musical genres, they felt the energy and creativity pulsating through the air, igniting their own passion for music and art.

As they explored the festival grounds, listening to a variety of musicians and bands, they engaged in conversations about harmony—a journey of collaboration, unity, and the beauty of blending different melodies into a cohesive whole. Alex spoke of the harmony he found in his art, combining colors, textures, and emotions to create resonant compositions. Sophia, too, reflected on the harmony in their relationship, moments of alignment and synchronicity that brought them closer together.

Yet, amidst the harmonies, discordant notes and challenges emerged. Alex grappled with creative blocks and the pressure to meet external expectations. Sophia faced moments of tension and misunderstandings, seeking clarity and understanding in the midst of conflicting emotions.

A weekend retreat to a music studio in a converted warehouse provided an immersive experience in the power of harmony. Surrounded by instruments and recording equipment, Alex and Sophia delved into collaborative songwriting and music production, allowing their individual talents to merge into a harmonious whole.

By a grand piano, they engaged in conversations about creating harmony—a journey of communication, compromise, and the art of finding balance. They spoke of the harmony they discovered within themselves, the strengths and vulnerabilities they brought to their creative endeavors, and the importance of embracing differences while working towards a common goal.

As they composed music together, their voices intertwining in melodic unity, Alex and Sophia felt a sense of synergy and connection. The harmonies became a celebration of their shared journey—a reminder that true collaboration required listening, understanding, and respecting each other's unique contributions.

Back in their apartment, they made a pact to nurture harmony in all aspects of their lives—to communicate openly and honestly, to celebrate their differences, and to find beauty in the harmonies they created together.

As the chapter drew to a close, a sense of unity and creativity filled the air—an invitation to join Alex and Sophia as they continued their journey of harmony, finding inspiration and joy in the city's melodies, and the harmonies they embraced within themselves and each other.

CHAPTER THIRTY-EIGHT
Resilience in the City's Challenges

In the city's array of challenges, Alex and Sophia discovered the strength of resilience—a steadfast determination to overcome obstacles, adapt to change, and emerge stronger from life's trials. The hurdles they faced in the urban landscape became opportunities for growth, learning, and the cultivation of inner strength.

A sudden city-wide power outage plunged Alex and Sophia into a moment of darkness and uncertainty. With no electricity to rely on, they found themselves confronted with challenges that tested their resilience and resourcefulness.

As they lit candles and gathered around a makeshift campfire in their apartment, they engaged in conversations about resilience—a journey of resilience, adaptability, and the power of perseverance. Alex spoke of the resilience he found in his art, using setbacks and limitations as catalysts for creativity and innovation. Sophia, too, reflected on the resilience in their relationship, moments of resilience and strength that fortified their bond.

Yet, amidst the challenges, moments of doubt and frustration emerged. Alex grappled with feelings of helplessness and the need to find solutions in the face of adversity. Sophia faced moments of vulnerability and the fear of not being able to control the uncontrollable.

A weekend retreat to a remote cabin in the mountains provided a transformative experience in the power of resilience. Surrounded by nature's rugged beauty and the simplicity of life off the grid, Alex and Sophia embraced the opportunity to reconnect with themselves and each other, finding solace in moments of quiet reflection and shared resilience.

By a crackling fire under the starlit sky, they engaged in conversations about cultivating resilience—a journey of acceptance, adaptability, and finding strength in vulnerability. They spoke of the resilience they discovered within themselves, the lessons learned from overcoming challenges, and the importance of leaning on each other for support during difficult times.

As they sat by the fire, sharing stories of resilience and moments of triumph, Alex and Sophia felt a sense of empowerment and unity. The challenges became stepping stones on their journey—a reminder that resilience was not just about bouncing back but also about growing, learning, and evolving through adversity.

Back in their apartment, they made a pact to embrace resilience as a guiding force in their lives—to face challenges with courage and determination, to learn from setbacks, and to emerge stronger and more resilient together.

As the chapter drew to a close, a sense of empowerment and growth filled the air—an invitation to join Alex and Sophia as they continued their journey of resilience, finding strength and wisdom in the city's challenges, and the resilience they nurtured within themselves and each other.

CHAPTER THIRTY-NINE
Discovery in the City's Secrets

In the city's hidden corners, Alex and Sophia uncovered the thrill of discovery—an exploration of mysteries, surprises, and hidden treasures that sparked curiosity and wonder in their hearts. The secrets that whispered through the urban landscape became invitations to unravel stories, unveil truths, and embrace the unknown.

A chance encounter with an old bookstore nestled in a quiet alleyway led Alex and Sophia into a world of literary treasures and forgotten tales. As they wandered through shelves lined with dusty books and antique manuscripts, they felt a sense of excitement and intrigue, eager to uncover the secrets hidden within the pages.

As they flipped through aged volumes and explored hidden nooks, they engaged in conversations about discovery—a journey of curiosity, revelation, and the joy of uncovering hidden gems. Alex spoke of the discoveries he made in his art, unexpected inspirations and revelations that fueled his creativity. Sophia, too, reflected on the discoveries in their relationship, moments of surprise and insight that deepened their connection.

Yet, amidst the discoveries, shadows of uncertainty and apprehension lurked. Alex grappled with the fear of the unknown and the desire to uncover hidden truths. Sophia faced moments of doubt and hesitation, unsure of what revelations might bring.

A weekend retreat to a historic museum filled with artifacts and relics provided an immersive experience in the thrill of discovery. Surrounded by ancient artifacts and archaeological wonders, Alex and Sophia embarked on a journey through time, uncovering stories of the past and unlocking secrets long forgotten.

By a display of ancient scrolls and artifacts, they engaged in conversations about embracing discovery—a journey of curiosity, courage, and the willingness to explore the unknown. They spoke of the discoveries they made within themselves, the revelations that brought new perspectives and understanding, and the importance of embracing uncertainty as a pathway to growth.

As they marveled at the museum's treasures and shared stories of discovery, Alex and Sophia felt a sense of awe and inspiration. The secrets became pathways to deeper insights and connections—a reminder that discovery was not just about uncovering hidden truths but also about embracing the journey of exploration and learning.

Back in their apartment, they made a pact to embrace discovery as an ongoing adventure—to seek out new experiences, to embrace the unknown with open minds and hearts, and to cherish the discoveries they made together.

As the chapter drew to a close, a sense of wonder and possibility filled the air—an invitation to join Alex and Sophia as they continued their journey of discovery, finding joy and inspiration in the city's secrets, and the discoveries they embraced within themselves and each other.

CHAPTER FORTY
Connection in the City's Diversity

In the city's diverse tapestry, Alex and Sophia discovered the beauty of connection—a weaving together of cultures, perspectives, and experiences that enriched their lives and deepened their understanding of the world. The diversity that flourished in the urban landscape became a celebration of unity, empathy, and the shared humanity that connected them to others.

A visit to a cultural festival celebrating the city's multicultural heritage immersed Alex and Sophia in a kaleidoscope of traditions, languages, and culinary delights. Surrounded by vibrant performances and displays, they felt the heartbeat of diversity pulsating through the streets, bridging differences and fostering a sense of belonging.

As they explored the festival grounds, sampling delicacies from different cultures and engaging with local artisans, they engaged in conversations about connection—a journey of empathy, inclusivity, and the power of building bridges across diverse communities. Alex spoke of the connections he found in his art, moments of inspiration and understanding that transcended cultural boundaries. Sophia, too, reflected on the connections in their relationship, moments of shared experiences and mutual respect that strengthened their bond.

Yet, amidst the connections, echoes of division and misunderstanding lingered. Alex grappled with the complexities of cultural identity and the importance of honoring diversity while navigating societal expectations. Sophia faced moments of cultural sensitivity and the need for open dialogue and empathy in bridging differences.

A weekend retreat to a community center dedicated to promoting cultural exchange and understanding provided an immersive experience in the power of connection. Surrounded by workshops, discussions, and performances highlighting various cultures, Alex and Sophia delved into conversations about embracing diversity—a journey of acceptance, curiosity, and the celebration of differences.

By a mural depicting unity and diversity, they engaged in conversations about fostering connection—a journey of empathy, understanding, and the willingness to learn from others. They spoke of the connections they forged within themselves, the lessons learned from embracing diversity, and the importance of creating spaces for dialogue and inclusion.

As they participated in cultural activities and shared stories with people from diverse backgrounds, Alex and Sophia felt a sense of unity and belonging. The connections became bridges to mutual respect and shared humanity—a reminder that true connection was about seeing the beauty in differences and finding common ground through empathy and compassion.

Back in their apartment, they made a pact to celebrate diversity as a source of strength and inspiration—to continue learning from diverse perspectives, to advocate for inclusivity and equality, and to cherish the connections they made with people from all walks of life.

As the chapter drew to a close, a sense of unity and solidarity filled the air—an invitation to join Alex and Sophia as they continued their journey of connection, finding beauty and inspiration in the city's diversity, and the connections they nurtured within themselves and each other.

CHAPTER FORTY-ONE
Reflections in the City's Mirrors

In the reflective surfaces scattered throughout the city, Alex and Sophia discovered the power of introspection—a journey inward that revealed hidden truths, untapped potentials, and the depths of their own souls. The mirrors that adorned urban spaces became portals to self-discovery, inviting them to confront their fears, embrace their strengths, and navigate the complexities of their inner worlds.

A chance encounter with a mirrored art installation in a bustling plaza led Alex and Sophia into a world of reflections and self-exploration. As they gazed into the mirrors that captured their images from different angles and perspectives, they felt a sense of curiosity and vulnerability, confronted by their own reflections staring back at them.

As they walked around the installation, observing how the mirrors distorted and reflected their images, they engaged in conversations about introspection—a journey of self-awareness, acceptance, and the courage to confront inner truths. Alex spoke of the insights he gained from introspection, moments of clarity and self-discovery that shaped his artistic vision. Sophia, too, reflected on the introspection in their relationship, moments of vulnerability and growth that deepened their connection.

Yet, amidst the reflections, shadows of doubt and self-criticism emerged. Alex grappled with insecurities and the inner critic that whispered doubts about his abilities. Sophia faced moments of self-doubt and the need for self-compassion and forgiveness in embracing her imperfections.

A weekend retreat to a meditation center in the heart of the city provided an immersive experience in the power of introspection. Surrounded by serene gardens and quiet meditation spaces, Alex and Sophia embarked on a journey of self-reflection, allowing themselves to delve into the depths of their minds and hearts.

By a tranquil pond, they engaged in conversations about embracing introspection—a journey of mindfulness, self-discovery, and the path to inner peace. They spoke of the insights they gained from introspective practices, the healing that came from confronting inner wounds, and the importance of cultivating self-love and acceptance.

As they sat in silent contemplation, their reflections merging with the still waters of the pond, Alex and Sophia felt a sense of clarity and serenity. The mirrors became mirrors of transformation—a reminder that introspection was not just about self-analysis but also about growth, healing, and the journey towards wholeness.

Back in their apartment, they made a pact to embrace introspection as a tool for personal growth—to set aside time for self-reflection, to listen to their inner voices with compassion, and to honor the insights gained from introspective practices.

As the chapter drew to a close, a sense of peace and self-discovery filled the air—an invitation to join Alex and Sophia as they continued their journey of introspection, finding wisdom and insight in the city's mirrors, and the reflections they embraced within themselves and each other.

CHAPTER FORTY-TWO
Resurgence in the City's Rhythms

Amidst the city's bustling rhythms, Alex and Sophia discovered the power of resurgence—a renewal of energy, passion, and purpose that breathed new life into their endeavors and aspirations. The rhythms that echoed through urban streets became a source of inspiration, guiding them towards resilience, creativity, and the courage to embrace change.

A spontaneous visit to a vibrant street market in a bustling neighborhood immersed Alex and Sophia in a symphony of sights, sounds, and aromas. As they navigated through the crowded stalls showcasing a kaleidoscope of goods and cultural treasures, they felt a surge of excitement and rejuvenation, invigorated by the lively energy of the market.

As they explored the market, sampling local delicacies and admiring handmade crafts, they engaged in conversations about resurgence—a journey of renewal, growth, and the capacity to bounce back from challenges. Alex spoke of the resurgence he experienced in his art, moments of reinvention and creative breakthroughs that propelled his work forward. Sophia, too, reflected on the resurgence in their relationship, moments of revitalization and reconnection that infused their bond with fresh vitality.

Yet, amidst the resurgence, echoes of stagnation and complacency lingered. Alex grappled with moments of creative blockage and the need to break free from routine. Sophia faced moments of restlessness and the desire to explore new horizons and possibilities.

A weekend retreat to a nature sanctuary on the outskirts of the city provided an immersive experience in the power of resurgence. Surrounded by lush greenery and serene landscapes, Alex and Sophia embarked on a journey of revitalization, allowing themselves to reconnect with nature's rhythms and rediscover their inner sparks.

By a tranquil stream, they engaged in conversations about embracing resurgence—a journey of transformation, renewal, and the courage to embrace change. They spoke of the resilience they found in moments of adversity, the lessons learned from setbacks, and the importance of staying open to new experiences and opportunities.

As they hiked through scenic trails and immersed themselves in the beauty of nature, Alex and Sophia felt a sense of revival and inspiration. The rhythms of nature became a metaphor for resurgence—a reminder that just as seasons changed and cycles renewed, they too could find the strength to rise again and embrace new beginnings.

Back in their apartment, they made a pact to embrace resurgence as a mindset—to welcome change with open arms, to seek inspiration from diverse sources, and to harness the energy of renewal in their creative and personal pursuits.

As the chapter drew to a close, a sense of rejuvenation and optimism filled the air—an invitation to join Alex and Sophia as they continued their journey of resurgence, finding inspiration and growth in the city's rhythms, and the resilience they nurtured within themselves and each other.

CHAPTER FORTY-THREE
Harmony in the City's Chaos

In the midst of the city's chaotic symphony, Alex and Sophia discovered the beauty of harmony—a blending of diverse elements, perspectives, and experiences that created a sense of balance, unity, and interconnectedness. The chaotic rhythms that echoed through urban streets became melodies of opportunity, collaboration, and the power of finding peace amidst turmoil.

A spontaneous visit to a bustling city square during a cultural festival immersed Alex and Sophia in a whirlwind of activity and diversity. As they navigated through crowds of people from different backgrounds, languages, and traditions, they felt a sense of awe and excitement at the harmonious blend of cultures and energies converging in one space.

As they explored the festival, sampling international cuisines, enjoying live performances, and admiring art installations, they engaged in conversations about harmony—a journey of unity, diversity, and the beauty of coexistence. Alex spoke of the harmony he found in his art, moments of synthesis and collaboration that elevated his creative vision. Sophia, too, reflected on the harmony in their relationship, moments of understanding and cooperation that strengthened their bond.

Yet, amidst the harmony, echoes of discord and tension lingered. Alex grappled with moments of conflict and the need to find common ground amidst differing opinions. Sophia faced moments of imbalance and the challenge of maintaining harmony amidst life's complexities.

A weekend retreat to a tranquil garden sanctuary nestled within the city provided an immersive experience in the power of harmony. Surrounded by blooming flowers, serene ponds, and harmonious landscapes, Alex and Sophia embarked on a journey of balance, allowing themselves to find peace amidst the chaos of daily life.

By a peaceful meditation spot, they engaged in conversations about embracing harmony—a journey of understanding, compromise, and the art of finding beauty in diversity. They spoke of the connections they forged with others, the bridges built through empathy and mutual respect, and the importance of fostering harmonious relationships in a world filled with differences.

As they sat in quiet contemplation, surrounded by nature's symphony of sounds, Alex and Sophia felt a sense of tranquility and connection. The chaos of the city became a backdrop for harmony—a reminder that amidst life's complexities, they could find balance and unity by embracing diversity and honoring the interconnectedness of all beings.

Back in their apartment, they made a pact to cultivate harmony in their lives—to approach challenges with empathy and understanding, to seek common ground with others, and to celebrate the beauty of diversity in their creative and personal journeys.

As the chapter drew to a close, a sense of peace and unity filled the air—an invitation to join Alex and Sophia as they continued their journey of harmony, finding beauty and inspiration in the city's chaos, and the connections they fostered within themselves and each other.

CHAPTER FORTY-FOUR
Serenity in the City's Storm

Amidst the city's bustling energy, Alex and Sophia discovered the serenity within—a calm center that remained steadfast amidst the storms of life. The storms that raged through urban landscapes became opportunities for resilience, growth, and the deepening of their inner peace.

A sudden downpour transformed the city streets into rivers of rain, washing away the dust and grime of daily life. Caught in the midst of the storm, Alex and Sophia sought shelter under a canopy of trees in a nearby park. As raindrops pattered against leaves and pavement, they found themselves enveloped in a cocoon of serenity amid the chaos.

As they watched the rain cascade down, cleansing the city with its gentle fury, they engaged in conversations about serenity—a journey of inner peace, acceptance, and the ability to find calm amidst life's challenges. Alex spoke of the serenity he found in his art, moments of clarity and inspiration that emerged from quiet contemplation. Sophia, too, reflected on the serenity in their relationship, moments of solace and connection that anchored them through turbulent times.

Yet, amidst the serenity, echoes of doubt and uncertainty lingered. Alex grappled with moments of insecurity and the need to trust in the process of growth. Sophia faced moments of fear and the challenge of letting go of control in the face of uncertainty.

A weekend retreat to a secluded cabin by a serene lake on the outskirts of the city provided an immersive experience in the power of serenity. Surrounded by nature's tranquility, Alex and Sophia embarked on a journey of inner peace, allowing themselves to let go of worries and embrace the present moment.

By the tranquil waters of the lake, they engaged in conversations about embracing serenity—a journey of surrender, mindfulness, and the art of finding stillness within. They spoke of the lessons they learned from nature, the wisdom gained from moments of solitude, and the importance of cultivating inner peace in a world filled with distractions.

As they sat by the lakeshore, watching the ripples on the water and listening to the symphony of nature, Alex and Sophia felt a sense of calm and renewal. The stormy skies became a canvas for serenity—a reminder that even in life's turbulent moments, they could find peace by embracing the beauty of impermanence and letting go of attachments.

Back in their apartment, they made a pact to nurture serenity in their lives—to practice mindfulness, to savor moments of stillness, and to trust in the natural flow of life's rhythms.

As the chapter drew to a close, a sense of tranquility and acceptance filled the air—an invitation to join Alex and Sophia as they continued their journey of serenity, finding solace and inspiration in the city's storms, and the inner peace they cultivated within themselves and each other.

CHAPTER FORTY-FIVE
Illumination in the City's Shadows

Within the city's labyrinth of shadows, Alex and Sophia discovered the light of illumination—a beacon of clarity, insight, and understanding that illuminated the hidden corners of their minds and hearts. The shadows that danced through urban alleyways became canvases for introspection, revelation, and the discovery of profound truths.

A late-night stroll through dimly lit streets led Alex and Sophia into the embrace of shadows, where the play of light and darkness created a mesmerizing spectacle. As they walked hand in hand, guided by the glow of street lamps and the shimmer of distant stars, they found themselves drawn to the enigmatic allure of the night.

As they wandered through alleyways adorned with graffiti art and whispered secrets, they engaged in conversations about illumination—a journey of self-discovery, wisdom, and the quest for deeper understanding. Alex spoke of the moments of illumination he found in his art, flashes of insight and revelation that inspired his creative process. Sophia, too, reflected on the illumination in their relationship, moments of clarity and connection that brought them closer together.

Yet, amidst the illumination, echoes of confusion and ambiguity lingered. Alex grappled with moments of uncertainty and the search for meaning in his artistic endeavors. Sophia faced moments of introspection and the challenge of unraveling hidden truths within herself.

A weekend retreat to a rooftop garden overlooking the city skyline provided an immersive experience in the power of illumination. Surrounded by the twinkling lights of the city below, Alex and Sophia embarked on a journey of inner clarity, allowing themselves to embrace the mysteries of the mind and the revelations that came with deep introspection.

By the starlit sky, they engaged in conversations about embracing illumination—a journey of insight, revelation, and the pursuit of truth. They spoke of the lessons they learned from moments of clarity, the beauty of inner transformation, and the importance of seeking wisdom in both light and shadow.

As they gazed at the cityscape below, bathed in the soft glow of night, Alex and Sophia felt a sense of illumination and understanding. The shadows became allies in their quest for truth—a reminder that even in darkness, there were lessons to be learned and insights to be gained.

Back in their apartment, they made a pact to embrace illumination in their lives—to seek knowledge, to question assumptions, and to always strive for deeper understanding in their creative and personal journeys.

As the chapter drew to a close, a sense of enlightenment and curiosity filled the air—an invitation to join Alex and Sophia as they continued their journey of illumination, finding clarity and inspiration in the city's shadows, and the profound truths they uncovered within themselves and each other.

CHAPTER FORTY-SIX
Reflections in the City's Mirrors

Within the city's maze of reflections, Alex and Sophia discovered the depth of introspection—a journey into the mirrors of their souls, where past, present, and future converged in a dance of self-discovery, growth, and transformation. The mirrors that adorned urban spaces became portals to inner worlds, reflecting the complexity and beauty of their inner landscapes.

A visit to an art gallery showcasing mirror installations immersed Alex and Sophia in a world of reflections, where every angle revealed a new perspective. As they moved through rooms adorned with mirrors of various shapes and sizes, they found themselves captivated by the interplay of light, shadow, and infinite reflections.

As they stood before a particularly large mirror that seemed to stretch into infinity, they engaged in conversations about introspection—a journey of self-awareness, reflection, and the quest for authenticity. Alex spoke of the moments of introspection he found in his art, glimpses into his own psyche and the layers of identity that shaped his creative expression. Sophia, too, reflected on the introspection in their relationship, moments of vulnerability and honesty that deepened their connection.

Yet, amidst the reflections, echoes of self-doubt and vulnerability lingered. Alex grappled with moments of insecurity and the fear of exposing his true self through his art. Sophia faced moments of introspection and the challenge of confronting her own fears and insecurities.

A weekend retreat to a secluded lakeside cabin surrounded by reflective surfaces provided an immersive experience in the power of introspection. Surrounded by mirrors that mirrored nature's beauty, Alex and Sophia embarked on a journey of self-discovery, allowing themselves to confront their inner reflections with courage and compassion.

By a tranquil pond reflecting the sky above, they engaged in conversations about embracing introspection—a journey of self-exploration, growth, and the courage to confront inner truths. They spoke of the moments of vulnerability they faced, the revelations that came with self-reflection, and the importance of embracing all aspects of themselves in their creative and personal journeys.

As they looked into the mirrored surface of the pond, seeing their own reflections intertwined with the beauty of nature, Alex and Sophia felt a sense of acceptance and wholeness. The mirrors became allies in their quest for authenticity—a reminder that by embracing their true selves, they could find strength and inspiration in their creative endeavors and relationships.

Back in their apartment, they made a pact to embrace introspection in their lives—to delve deep into their inner worlds, to confront their fears and vulnerabilities, and to celebrate the complexity and beauty of their true selves.

As the chapter drew to a close, a sense of empowerment and authenticity filled the air—an invitation to join Alex and Sophia as they continued their journey of introspection, finding wisdom and inspiration in the city's mirrors, and the reflections they uncovered within themselves and each other.

CHAPTER FORTY-SEVEN
Whispers in the City's Silence

In the city's moments of silence, Alex and Sophia discovered the power of whispers—a quiet resonance that spoke volumes, carrying messages of love, hope, and connection through the stillness of urban landscapes. The silence that enveloped busy streets became a canvas for intimate conversations, shared dreams, and the deepening of their bond.

A late-night walk through deserted city streets led Alex and Sophia into the embrace of silence, where the absence of noise allowed their voices to echo with clarity. As they walked side by side, guided by the soft glow of streetlights and the gentle rustle of leaves in the breeze, they found themselves drawn to the tranquility of the night.

As they meandered through empty squares and quiet alleys, they engaged in whispered conversations about the power of silence—a journey of intimacy, connection, and the language of the heart. Alex spoke of the moments of silence he found in his art, spaces of contemplation and expression that spoke louder than words. Sophia, too, reflected on the silence in their relationship, moments of shared understanding and empathy that deepened their connection.

Yet, amidst the whispers, echoes of longing and vulnerability lingered. Alex grappled with moments of yearning and the need to express his deepest emotions. Sophia faced moments of vulnerability and the challenge of opening her heart fully to love.

A weekend retreat to a secluded rooftop garden overlooking the city's skyline provided an immersive experience in the power of silence. Surrounded by the hushed beauty of nature, Alex and Sophia embarked on a journey of intimacy, allowing themselves to communicate through gestures, glances, and the unspoken language of the heart.

By a moonlit terrace, they engaged in whispered conversations about embracing silence—a journey of connection, vulnerability, and the beauty of shared moments of stillness. They spoke of the depth of their feelings, the unspoken understanding between them, and the importance of cherishing moments of quietude in a world filled with noise.

As they sat under a blanket of stars, their words mingling with the night breeze, Alex and Sophia felt a sense of closeness and tenderness. The silence became a sanctuary for their love—a reminder that sometimes, the most profound connections were forged in moments of quiet intimacy.

Back in their apartment, they made a pact to embrace the power of silence in their lives—to listen deeply, to communicate with heart and soul, and to treasure the moments of stillness that allowed their love to flourish.

As the chapter drew to a close, a sense of serenity and connection filled the air—an invitation to join Alex and Sophia as they continued their journey of whispered conversations, finding love and understanding in the city's silence, and the intimate moments they shared within themselves and each other.

CHAPTER FORTY-EIGHT
Echoes of Time in the City's Heartbeat

Amidst the city's rhythmic heartbeat, Alex and Sophia discovered echoes of time—a symphony of past, present, and future that resonated through the pulsating energy of urban life. The heartbeat of the city became a tapestry of memories, aspirations, and the continuous evolution of their love story.

A stroll through a historic district led Alex and Sophia to unravel the layers of time woven into the city's architecture and streets. As they walked hand in hand, guided by the echoes of footsteps that had traversed these paths before, they found themselves immersed in the timeless embrace of the past.

As they explored cobblestone alleys and quaint cafes nestled within centuries-old buildings, they engaged in conversations about the echoes of time—a journey of nostalgia, growth, and the interconnectedness of all moments. Alex spoke of the moments of timelessness he found in his art, capturing fleeting emotions and memories in his creations. Sophia, too, reflected on the echoes of time in their relationship, moments of shared history and dreams for the future that bound them together.

Yet, amidst the echoes, echoes of uncertainty and anticipation lingered. Alex grappled with moments of reflection and the desire to leave a lasting impact through his art. Sophia faced moments of anticipation and the excitement of what the future held for their love.

A visit to a historical museum showcasing the city's evolution over centuries provided an immersive experience in the power of time. Surrounded by artifacts and stories from different eras, Alex and Sophia embarked on a journey through history, allowing themselves to appreciate the interconnectedness of past, present, and future.

By a display showcasing old photographs and letters, they engaged in conversations about embracing the echoes of time—a journey of continuity, legacy, and the cyclical nature of life. They spoke of the lessons they learned from history, the wisdom gained from previous generations, and the importance of honoring traditions while embracing change.

As they stood before a mural depicting the city's transformation over time, Alex and Sophia felt a sense of connection to the past and hope for the future. The echoes of time became threads that wove their love story into the fabric of the city—a reminder that their journey was part of a larger tapestry of lives and experiences.

Back in their apartment, they made a pact to embrace the echoes of time in their lives—to cherish memories, to learn from the past, and to look forward with optimism and purpose.

As the chapter drew to a close, a sense of continuity and resilience filled the air—an invitation to join Alex and Sophia as they continued their journey through the echoes of time, finding meaning and inspiration in the city's heartbeat, and the timeless love they shared within themselves and each other.

CHAPTER FORTY-NINE
Harmonies of Change in the City's Melody

Within the city's evolving melody, Alex and Sophia discovered harmonies of change—a symphony of growth, adaptation, and the beauty found in embracing transformation. The city's melody became a reflection of their own journey, resonating with the rhythms of life's constant changes.

A visit to a bustling music festival in the heart of the city immersed Alex and Sophia in the vibrant energy of creativity and innovation. Surrounded by musicians playing a variety of instruments and genres, they found themselves swept away by the harmonies and rhythms that filled the air.

As they listened to the music that flowed through the streets, they engaged in conversations about the harmonies of change—a journey of evolution, renewal, and the endless possibilities that came with embracing new experiences. Alex spoke of the moments of change he found in his art, exploring new techniques and styles that pushed the boundaries of his creativity. Sophia, too, reflected on the harmonies of change in their relationship, moments of growth and discovery that enriched their connection.

Yet, amidst the harmonies, echoes of uncertainty and excitement lingered. Alex grappled with moments of artistic exploration and the thrill of pushing himself beyond familiar boundaries. Sophia faced moments of anticipation and the eagerness to see where their journey would lead next.

A chance encounter with a street performer playing an unfamiliar instrument provided an immersive experience in the power of change. Surrounded by the melodies of the unknown, Alex and Sophia embraced the harmonies of change, allowing themselves to be carried by the currents of transformation.

By a makeshift stage in a bustling square, they engaged in conversations about embracing change—a journey of adaptability, resilience, and the courage to step into the unknown. They spoke of the lessons they learned from embracing new experiences, the joy of discovering hidden talents, and the importance of remaining open to life's ever-changing melodies.

As they watched the sunset against a backdrop of music and laughter, Alex and Sophia felt a sense of freedom and possibility. The harmonies of change became melodies that enriched their love story—a reminder that growth and transformation were essential elements of their journey together.

Back in their apartment, they made a pact to embrace the harmonies of change in their lives—to welcome new experiences, to adapt to challenges with grace, and to find beauty in the evolving melody of their love.

As the chapter drew to a close, a sense of optimism and adventure filled the air—an invitation to join Alex and Sophia as they continued their journey through the harmonies of change, finding inspiration and joy in the city's evolving melody, and the endless possibilities that awaited within themselves and each other.

CHAPTER FIFTY
Embracing Serendipity in the City's Tapestry

In the intricate tapestry of the city's fabric, Alex and Sophia discovered the art of embracing serendipity—a dance of unexpected moments, chance encounters, and the magic found in the spontaneity of life. The city's tapestry became a canvas for serendipitous adventures, weaving threads of surprise and delight into their love story.

A leisurely stroll through a vibrant market on a sunny afternoon led Alex and Sophia to serendipitous discoveries—a quaint bookstore tucked away in a hidden corner, a street artist painting murals that captured the essence of the city, and a café serving aromatic coffee that beckoned them to linger.

As they explored the market's myriad offerings, they engaged in conversations about embracing serendipity—a journey of openness, wonder, and the joy of unexpected encounters. Alex spoke of the moments of serendipity he found in his art, chance discoveries that sparked new ideas and inspiration. Sophia, too, reflected on the serendipitous moments in their relationship, chance meetings and shared experiences that added magic to their connection.

Yet, amidst the serendipity, echoes of anticipation and curiosity lingered. Alex grappled with moments of excitement and the thrill of not knowing what each day would bring. Sophia faced moments of wonder and the joy of discovering hidden gems in the city they called home.

A spontaneous decision to attend a street festival celebrating local artists and musicians provided an immersive experience in the power of serendipity. Surrounded by the sights and sounds of creativity, Alex and Sophia embraced the serendipitous moments that unfolded, allowing themselves to be swept up in the spontaneity of the day.

By a stage where performers captivated the crowd with their talents, they engaged in conversations about embracing serendipity—a journey of spontaneity, joy, and the beauty of unexpected surprises. They spoke of the lessons they learned from seizing serendipitous moments, the connections made through chance encounters, and the importance of staying open to life's delightful surprises.

As they danced under the starlit sky, their laughter mingling with the music, Alex and Sophia felt a sense of freedom and adventure. The serendipitous moments became treasures that enriched their love story—a reminder that life's greatest joys often came when least expected.

Back in their apartment, they made a pact to embrace serendipity in their lives—to welcome unexpected moments, to savor the magic of chance encounters, and to find joy in the spontaneity of each day.

As the chapter drew to a close, a sense of wonder and gratitude filled the air—an invitation to join Alex and Sophia as they continued their journey through the city's tapestry of serendipity, finding beauty and excitement in the unexpected, and the endless possibilities that awaited within themselves and each other.

CHAPTER FIFTY-ONE
The Whispering Winds of Change

As the seasons changed and the city embraced a new rhythm, Alex and Sophia found themselves attuned to the whispering winds of change—a gentle reminder of life's constant evolution, the passage of time, and the beauty found in embracing transitions. The whispering winds became a metaphor for their own journey, carrying messages of growth, resilience, and the promise of new beginnings.

A weekend getaway to a quaint countryside retreat allowed Alex and Sophia to immerse themselves in nature's transformative power. Surrounded by rolling hills, rustling trees, and the soothing sounds of a nearby stream, they felt the winds of change brush against their skin, carrying with them a sense of renewal and possibility.

As they explored forest trails and meadows bathed in golden sunlight, they engaged in conversations about the whispering winds of change—a journey of transformation, introspection, and the cycles of life. Alex spoke of the moments of change he found in nature, the shifting seasons that mirrored his own growth and evolution. Sophia, too, reflected on the winds of change in their relationship, moments of adaptation and resilience that strengthened their bond.

Yet, amidst the whispers, echoes of reflection and anticipation lingered. Alex grappled with moments of introspection and the desire to align his actions with his evolving beliefs. Sophia faced moments of anticipation and the excitement of embracing new opportunities on the horizon.

A quiet evening by a crackling fire provided an intimate setting for deeper conversations about embracing change. As they watched the flames dance and listened to the wind rustling through the trees outside, Alex and Sophia delved into discussions about the winds of change—a journey of acceptance, growth, and the beauty found in transitions.

They spoke of the lessons they learned from embracing change, the strength gained from navigating life's twists and turns, and the importance of staying grounded amidst uncertainty. They marveled at the interconnectedness of all things, how the whispering winds carried stories of the past, dreams of the future, and the eternal cycle of renewal.

As they gazed at the starlit sky, their thoughts mingling with the night breeze, Alex and Sophia felt a sense of peace and serenity. The whispering winds became a source of comfort and inspiration—a reminder that change was not to be feared but embraced as a natural part of life's journey.

Back in their cozy cabin, they made a pact to embrace the whispering winds of change in their lives—to welcome new beginnings, to adapt to challenges with grace, and to find beauty in the ever-evolving nature of their love.

As the chapter drew to a close, a sense of harmony and renewal filled the air—an invitation to join Alex and Sophia as they continued their journey through the whispering winds of change, finding strength and resilience in life's transitions, and the endless possibilities that awaited within themselves and each other.

CHAPTER FIFTY-TWO
Shadows of Doubt, Light of Trust

In the midst of their journey, Alex and Sophia encountered shadows of doubt that tested the foundation of their trust. It was a moment of introspection, a pause in the melody of their love story where doubts cast fleeting shadows, only to be illuminated by the light of their unwavering trust.

The shadows of doubt crept in subtly, like wisps of fog on a cool morning, shrouding their hearts in uncertainty. Alex found himself questioning his decisions, his art, and whether he was truly living up to his potential. Sophia, too, grappled with doubts about their future, wondering if their dreams were aligned or if diverging paths lay ahead.

Their conversations turned introspective, as they sat under the canopy of stars, seeking clarity amidst the shadows. Alex opened up about his fears of falling short, of not meeting the expectations he had set for himself. Sophia shared her concerns about the unknown, about the twists and turns life might bring that could challenge their love.

Yet, amidst the shadows, the light of trust shone bright. They spoke honestly about their insecurities, their vulnerabilities, and the deep bond of trust that anchored their relationship. They reaffirmed their commitment to supporting each other through doubts and uncertainties, to communicate openly and honestly, and to trust in the strength of their love.

A serendipitous encounter with an elderly couple at a local park added depth to their reflections. The couple shared stories of their own journey, of the doubts they faced and the trust that carried them through decades of love. Their wisdom became a beacon of hope, reminding Alex and Sophia that doubts were natural but could be overcome with trust and communication.

As they walked hand in hand, the shadows of doubt began to dissipate, replaced by a renewed sense of clarity and purpose. They realized that doubts were not roadblocks but opportunities for growth, for deepening their understanding of themselves and each other.

Back in their shared space, they embraced with a newfound sense of trust, knowing that their love was resilient, capable of weathering any storm. They made a pact to face doubts together, to turn shadows into lessons, and to always trust in the enduring power of their connection.

As the chapter drew to a close, the light of trust illuminated their path forward—a reminder that doubts were fleeting, but trust was eternal, a beacon that guided them through the twists and turns of life's journey. And with each step, they moved closer to the culmination of their love story, filled with curiosity and anticipation for what lay ahead in the final chapters.

CHAPTER FIFTY-THREE

Whispers of Change, Echoes of Resilience

As the days unfolded, whispers of change lingered in the air, subtle yet undeniable. Alex and Sophia found themselves at a crossroads, where the echoes of resilience reverberated through their hearts, urging them to embrace the winds of change with courage and determination.

The whispers of change were like gentle ripples on the surface of a calm lake, signaling a shift in the tides of their lives. Alex felt the pull of new opportunities, creative endeavors that beckoned him to explore uncharted territories. Sophia sensed the winds of change in her own aspirations, a desire to pursue passions beyond the familiar.

Their conversations turned reflective, as they sat by the window overlooking the cityscape, watching as the sun set on one chapter of their lives, making way for the dawn of a new era. Alex spoke of his dreams, of the paths he wished to tread, and the uncertainties that accompanied change. Sophia shared her aspirations, the goals she hoped to achieve, and the excitement tinged with a hint of apprehension.

Yet, amidst the whispers, echoes of resilience resounded. They spoke of the challenges they had overcome together, the storms weathered and the growth that emerged from adversity. They found strength in each other's unwavering support, a foundation built on trust and love.

A chance encounter with a mentor from Alex's past brought clarity to their reflections. The mentor spoke of embracing change as a catalyst for growth, of facing challenges with resilience, and of the transformative power of determination. His words ignited a spark within Alex and Sophia, a renewed sense of purpose and determination to navigate the winds of change together.

As they walked through familiar streets, their steps echoed with a newfound resolve. They realized that change was not to be feared but embraced as a natural part of life's journey. They made plans and set goals, aligning their dreams with the whispers of change that stirred within them.

Back in their shared space, they stood together, facing the horizon with optimism and courage. They made a pact to embrace the winds of change, to adapt and grow, and to face the unknown with resilience and grace.

As the chapter drew to a close, the echoes of resilience lingered, a reminder that change was inevitable but their love and determination were unwavering. And with each passing day, they stepped closer to the final chapters of their love story, filled with curiosity and anticipation for the adventures that awaited.

CHAPTER FIFTY-FOUR
Unveiling Truths, Embracing Revelations

In the quiet moments of reflection, Alex and Sophia found themselves unraveling truths that had long been veiled, truths that brought both clarity and complexity to their love story. It was a time of introspection, of peeling back layers to reveal the raw essence of their connection and the revelations that awaited.

The veil of truths began to lift gradually, like a curtain unveiling a stage set for a grand performance. Alex delved into the depths of his emotions, uncovering layers of vulnerability and longing that had been masked by bravado. Sophia, too, explored the truths hidden within her heart, untangling knots of uncertainty and desire.

Their conversations turned introspective, as they sat in their favorite spot by the riverbank, the gentle flow of water mirroring the ebb and flow of their thoughts. Alex spoke of his fears, of the insecurities that sometimes clouded his vision of the future. Sophia shared her own vulnerabilities, the doubts that crept in during moments of quiet introspection.

Yet, amidst the unveiling, a sense of clarity emerged. They spoke honestly about their fears and desires, their dreams and aspirations. They found solace in each other's understanding, a comfort born from shared truths and a deep connection that transcended words.

A serendipitous encounter with an old journal brought unexpected revelations. The journal, filled with scribbles and musings from their early days together, served as a mirror to their journey—a reminder of the growth they had experienced and the love that had blossomed amidst challenges.

As they flipped through the pages, memories flooded back—moments of laughter, tears, and everything in between. They realized that the truths they had uncovered were not just about their individual selves but about the tapestry of their shared experiences, woven with threads of joy and resilience.

Walking hand in hand along the riverbank, they embraced the revelations that had surfaced, a renewed sense of understanding and acceptance filling their hearts. They made a pact to continue unveiling truths, to communicate openly and authentically, and to embrace the complexities of their love story with courage and grace.

As the chapter drew to a close, a sense of peace settled over them—an invitation to join Alex and Sophia as they embarked on the final chapter of their love story, filled with curiosity and anticipation for the revelations that awaited, and the culmination of their journey through love's intricacies.

CHAPTER FIFTY-FIVE
The Tapestry of Forever

As Alex and Sophia stood on the brink of their journey's end, they found themselves immersed in the beauty of a tapestry woven with the threads of their love—a tapestry that told the story of their growth, resilience, and unwavering bond. It was a moment of reflection, of looking back at the chapters they had written together, and the anticipation of what lay ahead.

The tapestry of forever unfolded before them, a mosaic of memories and moments that painted a vivid portrait of their love story. Alex traced his fingers along the intricate patterns, each thread representing a milestone in their journey. Sophia marveled at the colors that danced across the fabric, each hue symbolizing an emotion shared and a dream realized.

Their conversations turned nostalgic, as they sat in the garden of their shared home, surrounded by blooming flowers and the soft murmur of the breeze. Alex spoke of their first meeting, the sparks that ignited between them, and the slow burn of love that followed. Sophia reminisced about their adventures, the challenges they faced, and the triumphs that strengthened their bond.

Yet, amidst the nostalgia, a sense of curiosity lingered. They wondered about the chapters yet to be written, the blank spaces on the tapestry waiting to be filled with new experiences and shared memories. They spoke of dreams yet to be realized, aspirations yet to be pursued, and the infinite possibilities that awaited them.

A surprise visit from old friends added a twist to their reflections. The friends, who had witnessed the evolution of Alex and Sophia's love story, shared stories of their own journeys, the twists and turns that shaped their lives, and the enduring power of love in the face of adversity.

As they laughed and reminisced, Alex and Sophia felt a renewed sense of gratitude for the love and support that surrounded them. They realized that their tapestry was not just about their love for each other but also about the connections they had forged with family and friends, weaving a web of love and support that spanned generations.

Walking hand in hand through the garden, they marveled at the beauty of the tapestry of forever—a testament to their love's resilience, the colors of joy and sorrow blending seamlessly to create a masterpiece of shared experiences.

As they reached the end of the garden path, they paused, gazing at the horizon with anticipation and excitement. They knew that the tapestry of forever would continue to unfold, with new chapters waiting to be written, new adventures waiting to be explored, and a love that would endure for eternity.

With hearts full of love and gratitude, Alex and Sophia embraced the unknown, ready to write the next chapter of their love story—one filled with curiosity, twists, and the timeless beauty of a love that knew no bounds. And as they stepped forward into the future, their tapestry of forever continued to shimmer in the golden light of endless possibilities.

A Journey Of Love And Resilience

Dear Reader,

As you reach the end of "Long-Distance Love in New York," we hope you've been captivated by the heartfelt journey of Alex and Sophia. Their story is a testament to the enduring power of love, resilience, and the pursuit of dreams, set against the vibrant backdrop of New York City.

In closing, we invite you to reflect on the themes of communication, trust, and staying true to oneself that resonate throughout this book. May Alex and Sophia's love story inspire you to embrace life's challenges with courage and optimism, knowing that love knows no bounds.

Thank you for joining us on this enchanting adventure. We look forward to sharing more captivating tales with you in the future.

With warm regards,

Mikey Katodiya

Also by Mikey Katodiya

Love Stories Around the World
Long-Distance Love in New York

Standalone
Yesterday's Love Story

About the Author

Meet, who often goes by the pen name "Mikey," is a passionate writer who believes in the power of storytelling to inspire and heal. Writing has been his creative outlet, allowing him to explore complex emotions and share them with others. 'Yesterday's Love Story' is his debut work, born frompersonal experiences and a desire to connect with readers on a deeply emotional level. Meet hopes his words, written under the pen nameMikey, will resonate with those seeking solace and strength in the face of adversity.

Read more at https://www.instagram.com/bigpicstory.